An Enemy Among Them

Deborah H. DeFord
and
Harry S. Stout

Houghton Mifflin Company   Boston

Library of Congress Cataloging-in-Publication Data
DeFord, Deborah H.
    An enemy among them.

    Summary: A young Hessian soldier questions his
loyalty to his king after fighting with the British
in America during the Revolutionary War and spending
time as a prisoner in the home of a German American
family from Pennsylvania.
    1. United States — History — Revolution, 1775-1783 —
Juvenile fiction. [1. United States — History —
Revolution, 1775-1783 — Fiction. 2. German Americans —
Fiction. 3. Pennsylvania — Fiction] I. Stout, Harry S.
II. Title.
PZ7.D3617En   1987   [Fic]   87-3263
HC ISBN 0-395-44239-7   PA ISBN 0-395-70108-2

Printed in the United States of America
FFG 10 9 8 7 6 5 4 3

To our children:
Kimberly, Gabrielle, and Ethan DeFord
Deborah and James Stout

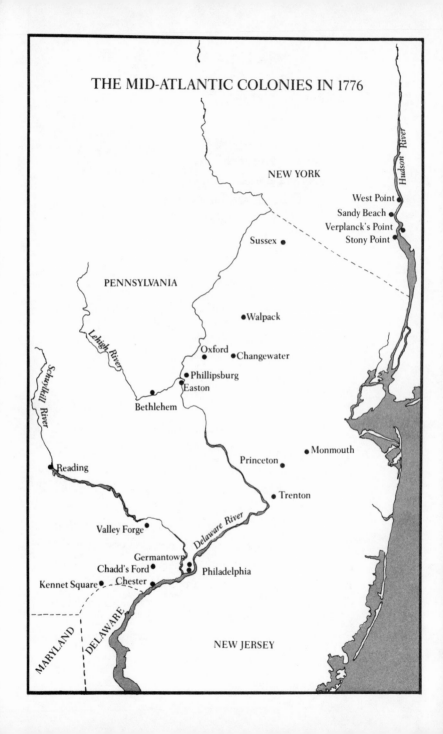

THE MID-ATLANTIC COLONIES IN 1776

NEW YORK

West Point
Sandy Beach
Verplanck's Point
Stony Point

Hudson River

Sussex

PENNSYLVANIA

Walpack

Lehigh River

Oxford
Changewater

Phillipsburg
Easton

Schuylkill River

Bethlehem

Monmouth

Princeton

Reading

Trenton

Delaware River

Valley Forge

Germantown
Chadd's Ford
Kennet Square
Chester

Philadelphia

MARYLAND

DELAWARE

NEW JERSEY

Prologue

The sea was still at last, after days of endless motion. Below deck, calm had replaced the cannonade of monstrous waves against the ship's hull and decks, and the young Hessian felt oddly unnerved by it.

He rubbed his hand over his forehead, tracing the knob that had surely grown larger since he last examined it. In the storm's worst pitching, every unsecured piece of baggage had flown through the air as though weightless, then smashed full force into walls, bunks, and cowering men. This soldier, however, had welcomed even the pain, because it distracted him for a moment from his terror and seasickness.

Now all had subsided — storm, sickness, and pain — and the sounds of human activity grew. One man moaned in his bunk. Another shuffled in search of the door. Yet another relit a lantern whose flame had been doused for safety's sake. By the flickering light he could see the storm's damage to the bodies and effects of the Hessian soldiers bunked in the ship's hold. The young soldier with the battered head looked from one comrade to the next, each bearing some mark of the ordeal — a ghastly pallor or a barely scabbed wound.

Were these really the same men who had marched for two hundred miles across Germany? He remembered them at the end of their trek, tired but proud and splendid, assembled as part of the Jäger Regiment von Knyphausen; and this ship, the *Mermaid*, waiting at dock with the other vessels that creaked and swayed in the water's low swell. Three hundred soldiers had crowded into the *Mermaid*, a ship built to accommodate one hundred fifty, ready to sail under the ensign of Germany's British ally, King George III, and swear allegiance to his cause — war against the rebellious colonies in North America.

Now in the flickering lantern light, as these months-old images faded once more, the Hessian searched for his knapsack. Inscribed on the back was C.T.S.M: Private Christian Theodor Sigismund Molitor. Christian's father had etched the leather with loving care. His trade was leather — he made shoes — and the knapsack had been his gift to his son. Christian found the pack and hoisted it to his shoulder, then pushed his way through the disarray of men and their jumbled belongings.

Once up into the air that blew fresh across the decks, he joined other men who massed topside in joyful relief at the storm's end. As he passed one pair of soldiers, he heard one of them speaking.

"Claus is gone," he whispered.

"Gone?" asked the other. "You mean he died of the cursed scurvy?"

"No, no," his companion said. "It was more merciful. He went overboard, in the storm."

Christian looked out over the eternal sea, rolling gray-green from horizon to horizon, and shivered. Would death in its icy embrace be such a mercy? Only by comparison, surely, with the torture of scurvy or some other ship-bound disease.

Bad enough for himself, Christian thought, and the Jäger corps on the *Mermaid*. Most of these troops were young volunteers. Christian thought back to his own leave-taking in Hesse-Cassel. The breeze had blown fresh in the sun of that day, too. His mama and papa alternately clung and pounded his back in wordless encouragement, while his younger brother watched with envy, and his baby sister hugged and kissed him with much laughter. Then he marched away, proud and happy. On other ships, however, sailed men who had been forced into service, or older men and officers who had brought along their wives and children.

At the bow of the *Mermaid*, a chaplain was reading aloud from his Lutheran prayer book, a prayer of thanksgiving. Another man passed around bowls of sauerkraut, peas, and hardtack, and cups of brackish water.

Meanwhile, someone had climbed the mast to the crow's next, and over a freshening wind, Christian could hear him calling from above. What did he cry? Was it possible, at last?

"Land!" Christian finally made out. "Land ho! Land!"

A hubbub swelled like the waves beneath the ship as one after another the soldiers heard and understood the long-awaited cry. They exploded into a single-hearted roar of cheers; they hugged and danced and laughed and cried. Christian raised his voice with the rest and, like the others, threw his hand skyward in a gesture of thanksgiving. Staring past his outflung hand, he saw a distant speck of motion above. A large bird climbed and soared — probably a land bird, he thought with a new thrill.

Yet at the same moment, an odd notion struck him: the bird was American; it was waiting and watching as the *Mermaid* drew near its home shores; and it knew, as Christian could not, what awaited the Hessian there.

Chapter One

I

The day before Christmas always lasted longer than any other day of the year for Margaret Volpert. It drew her out of a year of yesterdays into the magic of Christmas, with its pageant of colors and the sounds of people given over to enjoyment.

Even in this December of 1776, Margaret could close her eyes and breathe the scent of Christmas Eve — sweet and pungent as evergreens and warm wool — and she could almost believe that no black magic worked to rob the holiday of its wonder. Almost.

The candles were already lit by the time Margaret descended the narrow, turning stair to the large Volpert kitchen. Her mother, Anna Maria, and two neighbor women poked and stirred there at the huge fireplace, discussing the various treats they were tending in the suspended iron pots.

"Well, at last!" said Mama, as Margaret approached. She wiped the moisture off her wide, florid face with a corner of the apron that covered her girth. "And just in time. The men are wanting their ale, child."

She handed Margaret the tray of pewter steins while the other women smiled and fussed over her fine holiday clothes.

"*Danke schön.*" Margaret thanked her in the Americanized German they all spoke. She curtsied and turned away, more excited than ever. Her clothes *were* fine — more Christmas magic. She passed her young sister, Charlotte, on her way. Charlotte sat cracking walnuts and chewing on gingerbread with several other small children, giggling and hooting as the shells flew. The child's pale hair had already begun to fly free of Margaret's careful plaiting, but for once Margaret didn't mind. For the sake of that joyful face, she could even forgive her sister the day full of mischief she had carried on.

"I know why you're turning red," Charlotte had said earlier, when Mama called upstairs that the guests were arriving. She lay across her bed, never quite still, and let her head hang over the edge, so that she gazed at Margaret upside down.

"Lottie, if you don't *move*, Mama will cook you for dinner instead of the turkey," Margaret had answered. She grabbed her sister's jumper from the foot of her bed and tried to pull it over the little girl's head, tugging at the dress's long front laces, till Charlotte righted herself. Then she snatched up her hairbrush and used it relentlessly on Lottie's tangled blond curls.

"You're turning red," continued Charlotte between

6

clenched teeth, "because George Scheffer is right this very minute in our kitchen!"

"You're very silly, Lottie," answered Margaret. She straightened to her full five feet and handed her sister a pair of silk ribbons.

"Really? Then why does George spend so much time in our kitchen on bread day! And why is Jacob always mad as a caught bee?" Charlotte slipped away from Margaret's finishing touches like quicksilver. "Better hurry," she had added as she flounced out the door. "You're late!"

Now, Margaret winked as she passed the small children with her tray, earlier taunts forgiven.

The front room stretched long and whitewashed, with a dark timbered ceiling and four narrow windows across the front. At one end was a bed built into a cupboard and closed off by bright indigo curtains, where Mama and Papa slept. For Christmas Eve, the other end of the room was filled by a ceiling-high fir tree, dazzling with shining candles, gilded nuts and fruits, and gingerbread baked into a dozen fanciful shapes and sugared to make them sparkle.

The men sat on the straight-back parlor chairs with their feet stretched toward the wood stove. They were talking about the war, as usual. She circulated among them with the tray and served, listening absently while she searched the shadows for her brother Jacob and their neighbors George and Elizabeth Scheffer.

"I tell you," said Margaret's father to Dietrich Mumberg, another neighbor, "this war is getting much too close to Reading for comfort."

"Well, perhaps we'll stand a better chance to see Reading's young men again — including your John and our Nicholas," Carl Scheffer commented. He took a hefty swallow of the ale Margaret handed him, then slumped in his seat with a shake of his head. His scowl made him look more like his son George than usual.

"A lot of good that'll do us, when we lose our homes and land," Dietrich was saying. His face reddened as he spoke, and he mopped at it. "It's bad enough that the king is using his Redcoats to steal from us. But the Hessians! It seems as though every week another boatload of those miserable mercenaries arrives."

Margaret stood by the door with her tray. She'd heard this kind of talk many times in the last months, but still it held her like a bad spell.

"I hear they show no mercy," said Carl with another swig at his stein. "They care nothing for decency and honor — let alone women and children!"

"I don't want to see them either," Margaret's father, Frederick, interposed. "Still, many of the Hessians are the boys of our old neighbors in Germany. Some of them may even be cousins! Misguided, yes, but surely they can't be the monsters the English newspapers make them out to be!"

"Fah!" burst out Dietrich. "They're all that and worse! What kind of man fights wars just for the money? What have we ever done to them that they should sell themselves to the British against us? They'll take whatever they can get their greedy hands on and destroy the rest."

Margaret looked from one man to the next, all silent now. Her father stared into his stein, his long features drawn down and tight.

8

"Margaret," whispered Anna Maria behind her. Margaret jumped and turned. "Jacob and the others are ready for the children's treat. I need your help."

Anna Maria stood, wiping flour from her hands on her apron, ample and steady. On impulse, Margaret threw her arms around her mother's soft bulk and kissed her.

"What's this?" asked Anna Maria with a calm smile.

"I hate this war!" Margaret blurted out in a whisper. "I miss John."

"Tut, none of that. Not tonight," said her mother with a pat on Margaret's cheek.

The other women were shooing their younger children into the front room amidst much giggling and playful shoving. Margaret gave Anna Maria another grateful kiss, then let go. The time for Pelznickel, with his bag of gifts, had come at last. Time, too, to see George.

"Here, Margaret," said Anna Maria, handing her a bag full of warm sugared cakes and gilded nuts and fruit. "They're waiting for you outside the front door."

The evening cold had a sharp edge to it, as Margaret stepped out onto the small porch. Around the corner at the front of the house, Jacob waited in his costume. She wouldn't have known him — in oversized work clothes, a piece of chain around his ankle, and his face blackened and bearded — if she hadn't helped him with the disguise. But strange as he looked, the children inside would recognize him as their traditional Christmas visitor from the old country, Pelznickel.

Beside him, Elizabeth Scheffer smiled and greeted Margaret. She played the Christ-Child angel, the dispenser of blessings. Margaret hardly glanced her way. The third actor, sporting a donkey's tail and a mask with long ears, made her heart start thumping. Margaret slowed self-consciously at the sight of him; his mask hid even his eyes, but she knew it was George.

"Quickly, Margaret," hissed Jacob, reaching for the bag of sweets. "We're freezing out here!"

"Everyone's ready," she whispered. "Jacob, you be sure you don't hit anyone so hard they cry this year."

"That wasn't me," answered Jacob, "that was John. I was the donkey."

At the mention of John, his brother and sister stared at each other for a short moment. Then Jacob lifted his rod to bang loudly on the door. A chorus of squeals sounded from inside. He knocked again and the door was thrown open, revealing Papa in silhouette. Warmth and light fell across the lintel as he stepped aside to let the actors in. Margaret returned the way she had come, pausing to notice the fresh wet snow that had begun to fall.

II

Much later that night, the gifts long-opened and the festive meal a savory memory, Margaret quietly climbed the stairs to her room. She glanced around as she entered, hardly noticing the bright quilt burying her sleeping sister, or the heap of Lottie's day clothes on the floor. Her eye ignored the water-splashed washstand, and came to rest instead above the cedar chest, in the corner with the tallow lamp.

There hung the only extravagance of the low-ceilinged

room, a heavy, framed mirror. Stepping over her sister's clothes, Margaret stood before the wavy glass. She loved the white dress she wore — she had done all the embroidery herself, weaving dreams with every stitch through long winter evenings by the fire. The red apron matched her cheeks, and seemed to make her eyes bluer than ever; like her father and Jacob, she had narrow hands and feet and the extreme fairness of northern Europe; not like her mother and John, both broad and solid. Only those blue, blue eyes did all the Volpert children share. Now the magic of Christmas filled her with pleasure at her own slightness — filled her too with certainty that she stood on the eve of something more than just the holiday.

A small sound, barely louder than mice in the walls, came from across the hall. Margaret pulled the quilt from her bed and wrapped it around her. Then she tiptoed across the landing to her brothers' bedroom. In the dim wash of snow-light from the window, she could see Jacob, sitting cross-legged on his bed with his quilt pulled tight around his shoulders. He stared at the other bed in the room — John's bed, empty. Jacob sighed and his breath showed white.

"Jacob," whispered Margaret. He turned and saw her huddling in her quilt at the door.

"Come in and sit," he called quietly and moved to make room next to him.

"It's really snowing," she said, joining him at the window and firmly tucking her quilt over her feet.

"John's probably freezing in a tent right now," said Jacob. "Poor, poor John."

"I wish I were with him!"

11

"Oh, hush, Jacob!" said Margaret in a low voice. "I hate it when you say that. Papa needs you in the shop. We Volperts have done our duty with one of us in the war already."

The window sash rattled with a sudden gust of wind that blew wet snow against the small panes of glass. Jacob stared at Margaret in the pale blue light. Then he reached down into the narrow space between his bed and the wall. When he brought up his hand, Margaret could see that he held a musket. She breathed in sharply.

"Sh-h-h," Jacob hissed.

"Where did you get that?" she whispered urgently. "What are you doing with a thing like that?"

"The Widow Zeller has been paying me to split her wood. I bought this when they auctioned off that Loyalist Wenham's goods. The army needs weapons."

"Well, how is the army going to get this one?" demanded Margaret.

"I'll take it with me when I join!" he answered between clenched teeth. He gave her a long, searching stare. "You really don't understand, do you?"

"Oh, ja, I understand," she said, and her words seemed to spill from her mouth. "I understand that you're just like John. You want to run off and play with guns and knives when we need you here. All the boys are going! Why do you have to go too?"

"You're such a dumb girl, Margaret!" said Jacob. "You don't know anything at all! Papa says the English will make us slaves, just as we were in Germany. This is our land now.

We have our own government, our own churches, our own schools. If we want to keep them, we have to fight for them."

"Peter Lutz fought for them," Margaret insisted. "All he got was killed!" Jacob's gaze wavered for a split second, then he sat straighter, an odd picture in his quilt.

"Sometimes people *have* to die," he whispered, "so that the rest can live."

"You're just copying John!" Margaret whispered fiercely. "Anyway, Papa would never let you go!"

"Why not? He had a lot of soldiers in his family in Germany!" Jacob shot back. But Margaret could see the doubt in his eyes.

She shivered hard while Jacob carefully hid the untried weapon again. Then he was silent. Finally, he put his arm around her shoulders and gave her an awkward squeeze.

"It'll be all right, Margaret," he said. "You'll see. John will be safe, and so will I."

They shivered together as another blast of icy wind rattled the window. The huge maple standing sentinel outside swayed, and tossed its glazed branches till they clicked like a great collection of dry bones.

III

Christmas Day dawned wet and cold, and Private Christian Sigismund Molitor was drunk.

It wasn't the first time he'd been drunk in the weeks since he'd arrived in New York, but he felt sure it was the worst. His elbow scraped on the rough surface of the table, with his head planted dizzily on his hand. Two privates across the farmhouse kitchen raised tankards freshly filled with rum; the liquid spilled down their chins and onto their stained uniforms. Christian blinked hard, trying to focus, as the farmer's wife and daughter brought in large wooden trenchers of meat and roasted potatoes. Someone started the chorus of a familiar German Christmas carol, and the room filled with a bawling rendition of the song.

"So this is war," Christian thought. He shifted on his bench, carefully, for the sake of his balance.

Dreary daylight filtered in through the windows. The women must be serving breakfast, then, not supper. Fewer and fewer of the men around him were awake, sprawled on their beds of straw or slumped like him at the tables. He heard a burst of laughter and the movement of chairs from the next room where several officers were continuing an all-night card game.

Someone stumbled into Christian from behind, then laid a heavy arm across his shoulders. Christian's head fell off his hand and he barely saved himself from toppling.

"Need more rum?" asked the man, waving a bottle in front of Christian's face.

"*Nein*," Christian answered, and fought rising nausea.

"Me neither," nodded the other, but he continued swilling anyway, letting half the liquid soak into his dark, bushy mustache and dribble down his thick face. Christian had the sudden notion that the hair might crawl right off the man's lip, like a caterpillar.

". . . fight a *real* army," the man mumbled.

"I beg your pardon," Christian said.

"I said, I'd like to fight a real army," the man repeated loudly. "I'm tired of these puling, cowardly rebels, who don't have the courage to stand their ground."

"Oh," said Christian. His head slipped again and he decided to lay it on the table. The board under his ear seemed to resonate with the noisy, deep breathing that filled the room.

"They're no army at all," the soldier continued. "No regular uniforms, no drilling skills . . . they just skulk behind trees and fences and take pot shots half the time. When they're not running away, that is!"

"Oh," Christian repeated, his eyelids drooping shut.

"We'll be on our way back to Germany in no time," the man rambled on. "Meanwhile, they're somewhere over that river out there, in the blizzard, and we're safe in here. We can live it up!"

By this time, Christian could no longer hold his eyes open. He began to drift into a hazy dream full of rum and rebels. They drank and swore, and one raised his gun. Would he shoot?

Crash! went the gun's retort, and someone screamed. That scream jolted Christian back to reality, but it was no dream. It came from a snow-covered sentry as he burst into the room.

"The enemy!" cried the sentry as he dashed past the sleeping soldiers and into the room beyond. He blurted his message to the officers inside. "They're coming out of the woods to the north . . . *nein*, there are too many of them to be a raiding party . . . *ja*, some of them were detained

15

by the outpost — but others slipped right by . . ."

All around Christian, snorts and moans replaced the sounds of drunken sleep. The excitement that had rushed into the farmhouse with the sentry was as bracing as the bitter air that had followed him. Christian's mind groped for sense. The enemy? Was the man saying that American rebels were marching on Trenton, even in the storm that was now blustering in through the open door? Even on Christmas Day?!

The sentry suddenly reappeared out of the growing commotion in the next room. He left as he had come, not bothering to close the door in his hurry. Then Christian saw one of the regiment's captains emerge, dragging on his coat as he ran.

"To arms!" he roared to the men, who were just picking themselves up from the floor and benches. "To arms! We're under attack!"

The captain was quickly followed by several other officers, all in various stages of dress, pulling on ammunition belts and slinging their bayoneted rifles over their shoulders. Christian pulled himself to his feet and searched frantically for his own gear, trying all the while to clear his head. He threw on his uniform jacket, hoisted pack and rifle, and pulled his tall fur hat onto his head. As he pushed and crowded out of the farmhouse, he could see Jägers spilling out into the storm from buildings all up and down the Trenton street. What to do? Which way to go? If only he could think!

Then he was running, shocked and confused, after one wild glance at the Americans pounding down the lane in

16

determined pursuit. He heard their jeers and shouts, some shockingly in German, but he had no time to stop and think of that.

"Stop cowards!" they screamed. "Stop and fight!"

"Do Hessians always run from Americans?"

The enemy taunts were closing in. At any moment, Christian expected to be taken or killed. Then just ahead, he saw the Assunpink bridge. It waited, solid and unguarded, like a lifeline for the embattled Hessians. Christian and the others tripped over one another in their rush to cross.

Beyond the bridge, the Jägers regrouped, surprised that they had not been followed by the enemy. It soon became obvious, though, that their own number had been reduced by hundreds. Silence fell over the men as they formed up and moved swiftly along the highway, the Americans safely eluded at last. Christian's friend Heinrich Sotz came alongside him.

"They must have crossed the Delaware during the blizzard last night," he said quietly. Panic still showed in his heavy-lidded eyes.

"Well, they *still* didn't get us all," Christian countered. "They missed the bridge. They could have done it if they had secured the bridge first!"

"They only did so well because we were all drunk," Heinrich added. "And we were only drunk because of Christmas."

Christian glanced around him at the depleted troops, holding back fear and a sudden, grudging respect for the enemy's audacity. He swore under his breath, and pushed

17

the unwanted thoughts aside. His leather pack seemed to weigh heavier on his back, and he straightened his shoulders against its pull.

"Next time," he said aloud. "We'll see who runs."

IV

Margaret watched through the kitchen window as Jacob crossed the packed and dirty snow between the cowshed and workshop, then back to the house where she waited. He stomped in, knocking the snow off his feet on the way, and Margaret turned to him eagerly.

"Did you tell Papa?" she asked.

"Ah, Jacob," Mama interrupted from the fireside, "you're just in time to help."

"Mama," said Jacob with the barest hint of impatience, "I have to run some errands for Papa. I only came in for my scarf."

"It won't take a moment," answered his mother complacently. "If you'll just move the coals out of the bake oven, we won't trouble you further." She lifted the iron scuttle and shovel and extended them to her son with an affectionate smile and a quick pat on his arm.

"Jacob," Margaret interposed. "What did Papa say to the news? Is he terribly proud of John's victory at Trenton?"

"Of course he's proud," Jacob answered brusquely. "What else would he be? John's winning the war."

Margaret cast a startled glance at her brother as she made room for him at the brick oven.

18

The kitchen door was thrown open again, and Charlotte pushed in with her pudgy arms laden, leaving snow across the oak floorboards.

"Here's the butter," she said. She placed the crock on the table with a thump, and turned to leave again.

"Wait," said Mama. "What do you have in your apron pockets?"

"Nothing," answered Charlotte with a wide-eyed stare.

"Charlotte, it's a sin to lie."

"Oh, Mama," the child moaned. "It's just apples from the cold cellar."

"For shame, Charlotte Volpert! You know better. We must use our stores carefully. There's no telling how we might need them later, if the war doesn't end soon."

Lottie dug the apples out of her apron pockets and dropped them on the table. Margaret watched with her own fists clenched. They'd never had to scrimp like this before the war.

Jacob, meanwhile, had finished emptying the coal scuttle into the fire, frowning as he worked.

"I'll go now," he said. But just as his hand touched the door latch, Anna Maria called to him again.

"Ja, Mama," he said, with a touch of impatience. "Do you need something else?"

"Please drop Margaret at the Rapps' for me," she said.

"The Rapps'!" cried Margaret. A cloud of steam hissed in the oven as she swabbed it clean, like the sudden undoing of her fine mood. "But why? Haven't we a lot of work yet here?"

"Poor Elsa is down with the hollow cough, and I told her mama we'd bring her a cure today," answered Mama. She reached for a small fabric bag on the cupboard's highest shelf and held it out to her daughter.

"Mama, couldn't Jacob just run in and give this to Frau Rapp?"

"You can carry it in," insisted her mother, placing the bag firmly in the girl's hand, "and then sit with Elsa for a time while Jacob runs his errands. I'm sure your company will do as much as bark tea to cure her."

Margaret dragged to the door and pulled her cape off its hook.

"*Will* you hurry," said Jacob.

At that moment, someone knocked at the door. Jacob opened it to the smiling face of George Scheffer.

"Why, *guten Morgen*, George," said Margaret brightly, stepping back to let him enter.

"What a pleasant surprise," murmured Jacob.

"Have you heard the wonderful news about the Christmas victory at Trenton?" Margaret asked. "And then at Princeton a week later!"

"*Ja*," he answered, holding her gaze with his own. Then he turned quickly to extend a string-tied ham at arm's length toward Margaret's mother. "I brought your ham, Frau Volpert. It's all smoked."

"Thank you, George. You may set it here on the cupboard." Mama turned to her older son. "Jacob, I'm sure you should be on your way."

"Right," Jacob nodded. He hurried Margaret into her cloak and opened the door once more.

"Oh, are you going?" asked George. His first smile had dimmed. Now it disappeared altogether. He turned as though to follow them.

"George," said Mama. "I have something for your mother. Please wait a moment, won't you?"

Margaret's last glance, before Jacob pushed her out the door, revealed a dark-faced George — one they had all known to avoid when they were children — whose temper was obviously on the rise.

V

The streets of Reading were unusually busy that morning with people eager to be out and about their business while the sun shone. Jacob rode the Volperts' horse, keeping a slow pace on the slippery roads, with Margaret riding pillion behind him.

"George is stupid," Jacob was saying. "And you're stupid, too, if you think he's so great."

"Nice thing to say about your best friend, Jacob," replied Margaret, tartly. She watched the quick-stepping townsfolk without seeing them; instead, in her mind's eye, she saw George back at the house.

"He's not my best friend," said Jacob with feeling.

"Since when?" demanded his sister.

"Since none-of-your-business!" he answered curtly.

"Lottie's right. You don't like him coming to see me instead of you."

"Margaret, you are the dumbest girl I ever knew," exclaimed Jacob. "What do I care whether George visits you or not? Except," he added, "that George is poor company for any Volpert."

"What do you mean?" cried Margaret. When Jacob didn't answer, she kicked his leg with her dangling foot. "Come on, Jacob Volpert. You can't say things like that without explaining. What's wrong with George?"

"All right!" Jacob blurted. "I'll tell you what's wrong with your beau. He's a traitor, that's what!"

The accusation, made with such fury, left Margaret speechless. Once started, Jacob rushed on in a low voice. Margaret bent forward to hear him over the rising din down Market Street.

"He told me he won't take the Loyalty Oath to an independent America when he turns eighteen," Jacob began, "no matter how many Revolutionary soldiers or courts threaten him. He said King George deserves our first loyalty. And our soldiers are no better than rebels, so we're sure to lose."

"But even his brother is in the Continental Army!" cried Margaret. "And his father took the Loyalty Oath with Papa."

"I thought you weren't in favor of enlistment," Jacob retorted with some bitterness. Before she could answer, he added, "Anyway, George has been a royal courier. I think he figures on getting some high office later, if he sticks with the crown."

George, Margaret thought with a frown. George, who brought her sweets on market days, and always found an excuse for conversation after church; George, whose attention Mama minded, but only because "people talk."

I don't believe it, she thought and had taken breath to say so when a neighbor child came running and slipping past them, as though the entire British army were on his heels.

"Jacob! Margaret! You should see!" he cried between gasping breaths. "In the market square! Hurry!"

As he sprinted along his way, Jacob and Margaret noticed for the first time the great press of people ahead, milling and crowding about. All around them was a company of new Continental soldiers.

"What are the volunteers doing out there?" Margaret demanded, shuddering at the sight of them. "Are they forcing more boys to join?"

"They didn't force John," said Jacob as he nudged the horse into a cautious trot. "John wanted to go."

Close to Market Street, the crowd grew denser, and Jacob and Margaret had to thread their way carefully through standing carts and wagons. Then suddenly, they heard a dreadful cry just ahead, near the courthouse. Already the crowd had closed around them and Jacob had to stop for fear of trampling someone under his horse's hooves. Another scream pierced the clear air.

"What's happening?" cried Margaret. She clutched her brother's waist while she tried to see around him.

"I can't see!" he answered. He called to someone ahead of them. "Franz! Franz Miller! What is it? What's going on?"

A boy slightly younger than Margaret turned at the sound of his name. "It's Tom Warren," he returned in the American-style German of Reading. "His trial's ended."

"Tom Warren," Margaret said into her brother's ear. "The weaver?"

"Weaver and Loyalist." Jacob spat the word out like a bad taste.

The crowd barely parted in front of them and he pushed his horse into the breach. Just then, a procession appeared from around the north end of the courthouse. Another cry carried across the square, this time more of a moan, and now they could see its source. Standing in a wagon, with hands and feet tied, was a man entirely covered with black tar and goose feathers, some of which floated to the ground as the horse-pulled wagon lurched slowly along. The Continental soldiers surrounding the cart screamed and hooted at the figure, their derision sounding in stark contrast to Tom Warren's pitiful wails.

"They've done him, then," said Jacob grimly, as the watching crowd called out with increasing intensity.

"Traitor!"

"Tory!"

"Blackguard!"

They yelled till their voices were hoarse with venom.

"Oh, Jacob," mumbled Margaret, pressing her face against his wool jacket to hide her tears. "I feel sick."

"You'll feel a lot sicker," answered Jacob without compassion, "when it's George Scheffer you see in that wagon!"

He reined, then, and turned their horse away from the sight of the tortured man. They wove their slow way home through a sea of familiar faces turned suddenly terrifying in their belligerence.

Chapter Two

I

That morning left the taste of tar and menace in Margaret's mouth. Every day the flames of Reading's patriotism were fanned hotter, and so too was Jacob's determination to fight. Throughout the long winter, Margaret continued her impassioned debate with him over enlistment.

"Shoemaking is as important as fighting!" she would insist, as they scraped warm manure out of the shed. "The army wears out shoes faster than they can be replaced."

"Shoemaking is a good job for old men and children," he would retort, with a mighty heave of his shovel.

Another day she reported, "Conrad Heister died at Morristown of smallpox. I think more men are dying in camp than in battle."

"All the more need for new recruits," Jacob answered without hesitation.

"Jacob, they're freezing in their tents!" she cried.

"So?" he said, and walked away without another word.

Meanwhile, orders for army boots continued to pour into Papa's cobbler shop through the winter and into spring. They were orders he couldn't possibly fill. His chief apprentice had been his oldest son; while John served his country in uniform, Jacob made a poor and grudging substitute. No matter how late they worked, they simply got further behind.

"More prisoners were marched through town today," said Jacob at supper one summer evening. He put a large piece of pork in his mouth, then continued, waving his fork for emphasis as he spoke. "There were a lot of Hessian soldiers, too. They've set up a prison camp for them down by the river. People got upset about it. Some even threw stones at them."

"Jacob, your mouth is full," interrupted his mother. "Don't say another word until you've swallowed."

His frustration, never far below the surface, showed in the glitter of his eyes and his furious chewing.

"People can be so foolish," said Papa. "Persecuting the prisoners is hardly justice, whether or not they are our enemies."

"I'm not sure I blame them, though," said Mama. "At least, not entirely."

Margaret's food stuck suddenly in her throat.

"The Hessians are murderers and thieves," Mama continued. "They don't even know us, yet they help England try to destroy us!"

"You make it much simpler than it is, Anna," said Papa,

staring at her in surprise. "My own father was a Hessian in the Jäger corps. He fought with honor for his king and the allies of his king."

"That was different!" asserted his wife. Jacob and Margaret exchanged surprised glances, while Charlotte stared at her plate. They had never seen Mama contradict their father or raise her voice to him. "He fought European wars and European armies. The king's enemies were his enemies in truth."

"England and the German states are allies. For a Jäger in America, it is still a matter of fighting his king's enemies," said Papa with finality.

"*Nein*, Frederick, it is not!" said Mama with matching determination. "These Hessians are cruel and bloodthirsty, and they only care for what they can steal from the people they murder."

"That's ridiculous," cried her husband, putting his knife on the table with a loud clatter that made his children jump. "Many of those men had no choice about coming, would never have chosen to come. They fight out of duty, and you cannot fault a man for that."

"They may very well kill my first son," Mama burst out, noisily laying down her fork as well, and rising. "I can most certainly fault them for that! They should be shown no mercy." She paused then, visibly collecting herself, before continuing in a carefully controlled tone. "This business of placing them as prisoners in comfortable homes and making patriotic citizens feed and shelter them is criminal."

"If John were taken prisoner," replied Papa in a quieter

tone, "is that how you would like *him* to be treated?"

"It's not the same!" Mama said. She, too, had quieted, but her eyes flashed.

"Why is it not the same?" he asked, and he thrust out his jaw, clamping his mouth tightly shut.

"Because the Hessians are wrong," she said, "and John is right!"

Husband and wife glared at one another, neither willing to be the first to look away. Between them, the specter of their soldier son seemed to stand. At that moment, the latch lifted on the kitchen door with a click that sounded like a shot in the utter stillness that had fallen over the room. The door opened as though by magic, and John Volpert strode into the room.

There was a long moment of speechlessness; then John opened his arms wide and laughed.

"Doesn't a long-lost soldier even get a *'guten Tag'*?"

The family burst into whoops of joy and warm crushing hugs, all else forgotten in the happiness of the moment.

II

With John home and released from the army, the world came right for Margaret. Now they could be a whole family, a real family, once more. The war continued, of course, but it seemed to take a step back from Reading, despite the constant flow of rumor into Papa's shop that Washington and his Continental Army had moved from New York to Pennsylvania.

In fact, Margaret could almost imagine that there was no

war, as all the Volperts gathered for meals and resumed the normal routine of summer life, gardening and shoemaking, milking and haying.

Only Jacob's urgent interest turned every conversation to the subject of the Revolution. When Jacob wasn't plying John with questions he was ticking off the days until his birthday, when he could enlist.

"I never killed anyone," John replied one day to one of Jacob's questions. "I'm glad I didn't have to."

Margaret and her brothers walked through the peaceful countryside, spread with rolling green and gold hills around them.

"Would you ever have to kill someone?" asked Margaret.

Both John and Jacob stared at her in amazement.

"Rather than be killed myself?" John asked bluntly. "Or see one of my men killed? *Ja.*"

The young men talked on, but Margaret only listened in frustration. She wanted to object, or to make some telling point; but she could think of none. She adored John, huge and blond and even-tempered. She had always thought him impossibly strong and handsome. He seemed all the more so since his army duty. His hair was bleached white and his skin bronzed. He glanced at her and caught her adoring stare. In a gesture left over from their childhood, he bent suddenly, caught her at her waist and threw her over his shoulder.

"Put me down, oaf!" she yelled and pounded his back, happier than she'd been for months.

Jacob's birthday, when finally it arrived, dawned blue and clear, with a freshening north wind that blew away the heavy humidity of August. Margaret worked through the day with her mother and Charlotte, baking, and knitting the last rows on a pair of socks for Jacob. Periodically, she threw her arms around her young sister.

"Isn't it *wunderbar!*" she'd cry. "We're all home for the party!"

Dinner began with laughter and horseplay that was not easily stilled for Papa's prayer. But they had hardly finished the blessing when Jacob cleared his throat and addressed his family.

"Well," he said, breathless. "I've done it!"

He stared, unblinking, from one person to the next. Papa and Mama sat still, returning his gaze without comment.

"Done what?" asked Charlotte.

"I've enlisted, dummy!" Jacob retorted. "I've joined the army!"

Margaret laid her fork down carefully. This wasn't supposed to happen, not now that John was safely home. Margaret had counted on John to not let this happen.

All the while, John hunched his big frame over his plate, elbows on the table, hands folded and pressed against his forehead. Before he spoke, something in his posture warned Margaret of what was coming. The room seemed to dim, as though a cloud had passed in front of the sun. She shivered, suddenly, though the breeze through the kitchen was warm.

"I'm going, too," he said at last, and he raised his chin in a gesture both calm and decided. "I re-enlisted when Jacob joined. We'll serve together, with General Anthony Wayne and the Pennsylvania regiment."

"No!" cried Margaret. "No! No!"

Then she covered her face with her apron, while all her store of helpless rage welled up in awful sobs.

A week later, Margaret could only watch and cry again as her brothers trundled out of Reading in a wagon full of recruits, and wonder what would come of it all. Certainly, if it didn't save them, it would destroy them.

III

Christian Molitor shrugged his pack onto his back with a sigh and a last glance around the clearing. Every surface wore the sheen of early morning dew, and a mist played among the trees.

"Look at it this way," said Heinrich Sotz. "We may see some *real* action again. It's got to be better than this game of cat and mouse General Knyphausen's been playing with the rebels."

"Hm-m," answered Christian, as he scanned the Stirn Brigade around him. He ran a hand across his sweating forehead and followed Heinrich to the gathering of their company on the Lancaster road, in this place called Delaware. He sighed again. "The Americans are just such a mess," he said. "No uniforms. No order. Why aren't we beating them?"

Heinrich shook his head, a sober expression on his young features. Then he brightened.

"Hey, I didn't tell you! I picked something up for us in Newark." He reached into a bag slung from one shoulder and pulled out a glass flask. "Rum," he said with a twitch of his eyebrow and a glint in his eyes. He shook it once at Christian, then replaced it quickly as their captain appeared for a last inspection before they abandoned the camp.

"That's great, friend," answered Christian, without enthusiasm. He moved into line and faced north with the rest — north for Pennsylvania.

"What's wrong with you?" demanded Heinrich, coming alongside with a lopsided smile. "Miss your mother?"

It was a standard camp joke, but Christian didn't smile in return.

"Maybe I do," he said. The captain gave the order to march and the drummer began his steady timekeeping work. Heinrich watched Christian for a moment, as they marched out, side by side. Then he shook his head again with his one-sided smile back in place.

"*Ja,*" he said. "So do I."

At the top of the rise, the trees thinned for a short stretch. The patchwork terrain of rich farmland that stretched amid vast spreads of heavy forest reminded Christian poignantly of home. In truth, he *did* miss his family, his quiet life as a shoemaker, his friends in Hesse.

"Why do they fight so hard?" Christian blurted suddenly. "Don't they know they're just a mob against the strongest armies in the world?"

"Not a mob," corrected Heinrich. "If that were all, we'd have been through six months ago. They're determined and methodical. We won't see home for a while yet."

"Have you ever thought of running?" Christian asked, lowering his voice. He swatted at the flies that worried his neck and ears. "Maybe stowing away on some ship bound for home?"

Heinrich stared at him, startled. Then he shook his head.

"You just need some sleep," he said. "And a good, honest fight."

The glare of sun on water ahead blinded Christian for a moment. According to the captain, they were crossing the White Clay Creek that ran for some distance between steep rocky walls.

"I hear the Americans held this ravine," commented Heinrich, as they approached.

"Why'd they leave it?" asked Christian. He followed his friend along the narrowing path uneasily.

"Who knows?" Heinrich replied, then laughed. "Maybe they knew something we don't."

Christian felt a prickling up his scalp and arms as the full press of troops crammed into the channel. *Like a fox in a trap*, he thought. *We could be destroyed in here.*

Unwanted memories of Trenton crowded the concentration he needed to keep up the pace over the troublesome rocks. The commotion of the troops' movements would certainly mask any warning sounds, should danger be poised among the surrounding cliffs. Christian stole sharp-eyed glances up the rocky walls, searching for any gleam of metal or color.

For half an hour they trudged through the difficult terrain. By the time they finally left the pass and moved cautiously into the open again, Christian could have collapsed with the relief to his overtaut muscles and nerves. But no incident occurred. The tension simply added to the tedium of weeks of marching.

IV

The Stirn Brigade stayed in their next camp just long enough for cleaning weapons and inspection, and only the unexpected arrival of a civilian rider distinguished it from a hundred other camps. At the last possible moment, Christian had one brief glance at the stranger's face — fair-skinned like most of the German troops but without their typical mustaches and tightly tied queues — before he rode swiftly past the clustered troops to the officers' tents. The stranger was American. The casual unkemptness of both his clothes and his posture gave him away. As Christian and the others readied themselves for another day's trek, Christian wondered about the man. But not for long. Nothing held Christian's interest for long these days.

They set out once more on a two-day march along the overland road, moving steadily toward Chester County, south of Philadelphia. A strong pocket of American resistance had been reported, the captain said, around the Brandywine Creek.

"Do you think that stranger last night brought the information?" Christian asked Heinrich as they marched.

"Who knows?" Heinrich answered with a shrug. "What difference does it make? What matters is that now we get our chance!"

"*Ja!*" added another man. "And this time, we'll destroy them!"

34

"The way we did at Trenton?" Christian murmured to Heinrich. "We might as well start running in the other direction now, and save ourselves the march."

Heinrich missed his step, and stared at his friend with a baffled, angry frown.

"You're a Jäger!" he hissed through clenched teeth. "Act like one."

Heinrich's comment felt like a slap in the face. Christian marched on, staring fixedly ahead, with a pain in his chest. But as he marched silently through the afternoon and into the evening, he knew the jibe hurt because it hit the mark. He tried to conjure up fantasies of a triumphant homecoming to Hesse, wearing the laurels of victory, the kind of dream he'd had before he ever saw this cursed place. Certainly he was a Jäger! Of course they would win!

But with sunset, Christian's efforts bogged down again, caught like his feet in the marshy, confusing woodlands through which the army now slogged.

"Do you think anyone knows where we are?" Heinrich asked once, picking himself up from one of countless falls among the thick tangle of tree roots and brambles. Christian swatted helplessly at the swarming armies of mosquitoes.

"I don't care," he muttered. He swore as a long, thorny branch scraped across his face. "I just want to get through it to somewhere else."

The eerie flicker of fireflies danced all around them.

"Remember when the others told us those were wood spirits?" Heinrich asked. "We were scared to death!"

"I remember," said Christian. "We didn't know what fear was."

35

Sometime before dawn, the Hessians came clear at last of the forest's menace and made their morning bivouac. Christian collapsed in the shade of a giant walnut tree. He woke to eat, then dozed off again, and didn't fully revive until Heinrich shook him awake with news. The Americans had actually been scouted out along the Brandywine Creek at a place called Chadd's Ford! After that, sleep was impossible. When the brigade fell once more into marching rank, it was to the midnight music of peepers and night birds rather than fife and drum. Heinrich stared at him through the purple gloom, even went so far as to slap his shoulder, but said nothing.

They reached the Brandywine before morning, keeping well back and silent. At daybreak, the muffled sound of a wet drum beating out reveille echoed from across the stream. The Americans were over there, but they were invisible, as were the river and its banks, all shrouded in eerie, sound-distorting fog. It played on Christian's mind as he and his company ate a hasty, cold breakfast. He began to see things that weren't there, to hear sounds that were nothing but his own heartbeat.

"Spooky, huh?" intoned Heinrich, in a sepulchral whisper.

"Sh-h-h!" hissed their captain. "Not a sound!"

Shortly after, Christian's company moved forward. They were the fake attack at Chadd's Ford, responsible to fire on the Americans across the river and to divert their artillery and attention away from the surprise attack from behind. Some of the company had complained. They wanted to be in on the real action. As far as Christian was concerned, his assignment would bring him close enough.

"Ready!" the captain said in a throaty whisper. Christian lifted his musket and took aim at the glaring white space before him, his finger tight on the trigger, his belly tight as well.

"Fire!" shouted the captain, letting off his gun in a blast that shattered the muffled stillness. A thousand blasts followed, then more and more. And then Christian could hear artillery from the other side. The enemy was engaged, at last!

The firing continued for an hour, while the fog burned off. And then for another hour. And another. Not until midafternoon did the American troops finally start shifting positions. Christian could see their reinforcements joining the main body of fighting men, trying to shore up their defense as though it were a breaking dam. But then he saw the German troops as well, moving up behind and from the sides — the surprise attack! The American activity was too late. They'd been fooled and the battle was virtually over.

Abruptly, Christian's division received orders to cease fire and march ahead. No more holding off now — the time had come. With grim determination that fought off his panic, Christian followed Heinrich into the cool waters of the Brandywine. For a moment all was quiet.

"Hey, Private," said Heinrich over his shoulder to Christian, "how about a little swim before . . ."

He was interrupted by a sharp crack. Christian's head flew up in time to see his friend clutch at his throat and reel over backwards. Then suddenly, all was shattering noise and chaos.

For one brief moment, Christian stood paralyzed, staring at the bubbling water. Then the order came from behind.

"He's dead. Leave him there. Move ahead! Move!"

Blindly, Christian staggered ashore and up the embankment where the Americans fired furiously at the invading forces. He scrambled through thorns and underbrush, up the hill with his bayonet fixed. The battle was joined in earnest, a deadly struggle amid pandemonium, gunfire, and wrenching cries for help.

"I'm hit! Please help me! I'm dying!"

Not far from Christian, an ammunition wagon exploded and instantly created a blast furnace that sucked the air out of his lungs and seared his face. All around him the musketry roared. The entire riverbank was a mass of flame and smoke and falling soldiers.

What followed was hellish confusion. The Americans, with nowhere to run, and hopelessly outnumbered, fought with their bayonets and broadswords like men possessed.

Why don't they quit? Christian wondered in barely checked panic.

He watched one after another of his friends fall, and surely twice that number of Americans were down. He raised his face to heaven and his silent cry went up — *I don't want to die!* At the same moment, out of the corner of his eye he saw an American coming at him. He wheeled, gun at the ready, and heard an appalling shriek as the blade of his bayonet sliced into the man's middle. The look of terrified hate that contorted the man's face gave way to the soft features of a young soldier.

Just like me, Christian thought in that split second. *He's just like me.*

Slowly the American sank to the ground, whimpering in

German — yes, German! It sounded to Christian as though he was asking for his brother, but no other Americans were around. Then he fell to the ground.

Christian stared wildly in every direction, tears of rage and frustration streaming down his face.

In that moment of distraction, Christian saw another flaming ammunition wagon rolling toward him, ready to explode. Too late, he tried to run, but just when he might have saved himself, the sharp pain of a musketball seized his leg. The blasted limb buckled beneath him at the same moment that his ears were shattered by a crash. Then a great sheet of fire erupted around him. For one second, Christian saw the flash and felt the clothes burning off his back.

Why me? Christian thought. *Why are they trying to kill me?*

Then thought ceased.

V

For days, the talk in Reading had been full of the battle at Brandywine Creek, and every visitor to the Volpert house brought more rumor and speculation, till Margaret thought she would go wild.

"They say it was brutal for our men," Dietrich Mumberg reported, standing on the porch with Papa.

"Was General Wayne involved?" Margaret's father asked.

"Oh *ja!* He was the hero, he and his men. They saved the rest of the army by fighting while the others retreated."

General Wayne! thought Margaret. That was her brothers' commander!

"Any news of the men?" Frederick asked quietly.

"*Nein*, Frederick," answered his friend. "There was too much confusion. I'm sorry."

Finally, the worry and suspense were too much, and Margaret begged the job of marketing. Winding her way through Reading's streets, she gazed at the many strange faces filling the town. Many were British and Hessian prisoners, newly arrived.

And the American soldiers! Their uniforms hung ragged on gaunt frames — some men on foot, others riding, all of them exhausted from the long months of fighting on inadequate provisions. Margaret anxiously searched the faces of the young men she passed for either of her brothers. Many of them returned her interest, leaving her flustered but determined to continue.

"Margaret! Wait!"

Margaret's heart thumped in a moment's wild hope at the sound of the man's voice behind her. She whirled, only to see George Scheffer pressing toward her through a crowd of English prisoners.

"*Guten Morgen*, Margaret," he said. "I haven't seen you for a while."

"We've all been rather busy," said Margaret tersely, and looked away to hide the disappointment that must be obvious. "Anyway," she continued, as they began to walk, "you see me every Sunday . . . in church."

"Across the room," added George. He took her hand, suddenly, and tucked it under his arm.

"Margaret," he said, slowing their pace. "Have I offended you somehow?"

"George, please," Margaret began, and tried to free her hand.

"Because if I have," he continued, "I wish you'd tell me and at least let me apologize." He stopped altogether and turned to face her, but she stared resolutely over his shoulder, at the passers-by, at the ground, at the tavern door beside them. Until this moment, she hadn't realized how thoroughly her feelings for George had cooled. "I want to see you more," he finished in a tone that was almost menacing.

"George, I really . . ." said Margaret, jerking her hand free at last. "Please excuse me."

Without thinking what she was doing, Margaret hurried up the tavern steps and through the door. Just inside, she tripped and stumbled into the lap of a man sitting at the nearest table.

He grabbed Margaret to stop her fall, then held her still while he examined his catch. With a shock, she recognized his British officer's uniform. His face creased into a sudden, disturbing smile.

"Well, now," he said. "This is something else altogether."

Margaret didn't understand the officer's English, but his intent was clear and frightening. Hateful regulations that allowed these prisoner-officers such freedom! She tried to pull away, but he held tighter. In alarm, she struggled harder, and the man began to laugh. The cheers and hoots of the men around them mingled with her own frightened whimper.

Margaret's frenzy was edging toward terror, when into the fray stepped George — calm and dignified. He spoke quietly to the officer, in English, gesturing to Margaret, the foreign words tumbling from his mouth. The man straightened as he listened, inclining his head and looking from Margaret to George. When George stopped speaking, the man loosened his grip on his captive, then helped her stand. He said something politely to each of them and gave a small bow. At the same time, George led Margaret outside. As they crossed the threshold into the bright light of noon, a deep burst of laughter rolled out of the dark doorway.

"George," said Margaret slowly, as they descended the tavern steps. "What did you say to him?"

"Nothing much," George answered. "I just explained that you belong to a solid Reading family, and that he would be wise to treat you with more courtesy."

George's eyes came to rest on Margaret's and this time she returned his stare. There was something indefinable in those eyes, something hidden and distant. Despite the rescue, for which Margaret was sincerely grateful, they did not encourage trust.

Just then, a familiar voice called out from along the street. "Margaret!"

George and Margaret turned to see who called and cried out in unison,

"Jacob!"

Jacob strode along the street, looking like a scarecrow come to life. Margaret ran to him, and he threw his arms around her, hugging her close against his filthy uniform. She didn't care about the dirt or the smell, only clung with all her strength. After a joyful moment, she realized that Jacob had become still. He had just noticed George Scheffer.

"Welcome back, Jacob," said George.

Jacob didn't answer, his expression unreadable.

"Jacob," Margaret quickly interposed. "George just helped me in the most amazing way."

"Did he," said Jacob flatly.

Margaret described the episode, leaving out her reason for entering the tavern in the first place. The quieter Jacob became, and the steadier his gaze, the more she chattered. Finally George interrupted.

"The English aren't so bad," he said. "The man meant no harm. As a matter of fact, most of them are gentlemen."

"Gentlemen! Let me tell you about English gentlemen —" Jacob spat out, then immediately cut himself off. "Excuse me. Never mind."

Jacob offered his hand to George, his face stony.

"I owe you my thanks for taking care of my sister," he said.

George wavered only a moment, then reached out and accepted the hand.

"My pleasure," he said in a subdued voice. He stepped back a pace. "You must excuse me. I'm expected."

As he walked away, Jacob turned to Margaret.

"I'm glad you're all right," he said and hugged her close again. "Now tell me, please, just what you were doing in a tavern by yourself?"

"Where's John?" she demanded. Jacob opened his mouth to speak, then closed it again. Then he sighed deeply.

"He's wounded, Margaret," he answered finally. "Wounded bad. But he's still alive and probably in a hospital by now — maybe at Bethlehem. I saw him in a caravan of wagons that carried the dead and wounded soldiers away from Brandywine. I wanted to stay with him but they wouldn't let me. Right now, General Wayne is reorganizing our regiment. I'm only here in search of supplies."

Margaret walked beside Jacob without a glance at the people around them. No use now to look for John's face among the crowds. She clung to Jacob's arm, thankful for the feel of it. Then Jacob blurted out, "Oh Margaret, how could I have ever wanted to fight? It was awful! I hate it. The whole battle, I was frightened to death. I'm afraid to go back."

Margaret held tight and nodded, trying to think past the horror of John being wounded.

"It's all right to be afraid," she said, tentatively. "You fought bravely and did all you could." She laid her head, for a moment, against his shoulder. "I'm proud of you."

Chapter Three

I

Mama took one look at Jacob and knew the news was bad. His eyes spoke without his saying a word. Charlotte ran for Papa, and the Volperts assembled as they had at John's homecoming, only solemn now instead of joyful.

"What have the Hessians done to my son?" demanded Mama.

Jacob hedged. "Mama, it's England we're fighting."

"Tell me," she said.

As Jacob recounted the battle story and then described John's stomach wound, his mother grew still, her eyes unfocused. Meanwhile, the fear Jacob had earlier confided to Margaret disappeared beneath his story of the brave Americans. They didn't win, he said, but they didn't run, either.

"The army is done in, though," he continued. He stuffed a potato dumpling into his mouth whole, hardly chewing before he swallowed it and took another. "And I have a day to gather as much as I can. We need everything — bread, meat, clothes, ammunition . . ."

"And shoes," finished Papa with a sigh. "Always shoes. With a dozen shoemakers in this town, we cannot keep up with the demand."

"*Ja, ja*," Mama cut in suddenly. "But tell me again about John."

"Jacob has told us about John already," snapped Papa. "John is hurt but he's alive. What more can the boy say?"

"Are you sure he's been taken to Bethlehem?" she asked her son.

"No, Mama," answered Jacob. "But I know a lot of men have gone there. The Moravian hospital is one of the biggest available right now."

"If only he hadn't re-enlisted!" cried Margaret.

Jacob fixed a pained, blue gaze on his sister.

"Are you blaming me?" he asked.

"You!" she repeated in surprise. "No . . . I . . ."

"Just how close are the British forces, son?" asked Papa.

"Howe is moving them closer, Papa," said Jacob. "But he's moving slowly. General Washington has troops between the enemy and Reading."

"But the British are practically here," murmured Papa. "How did such a thing happen?"

"Papa, there are so *many* of them," Jacob answered, his eyes suddenly haunted. Then he raised his chin in a typical Volpert gesture. "But they're no better than our men. We fought them teeth to teeth and we were as strong as any of them — and braver than some."

"Aa-ah," sighed the older man, with a proud squaring of his shoulders. "That is all we need. They fight on our sod. We fight for freedom!"

"That's all very well," said Mama, shortly, as she stood. "But what about John!"

"Well, Anna, what about him?" questioned Papa sharply. "I can't make him well while he's thirty miles away."

"No, you can't," answered his wife. She placed her fists on her broad hips and added, "But I can!"

"I'll have none of your powwowing with your friends, Anna Maria," he said sternly.

"We made the Lutz girl better with a potion and a spell."

"Anna, I mean what I say," intoned Papa.

Charlotte slid silently down from her stool and wandered from the room. As Margaret hurried to clear the table, she wished she could do the same.

"I forbid it," Papa was saying. Mama pursed her lips and stared for a moment at her husband.

"All right," she said. "I won't powwow."

"You certainly won't," Papa agreed with a mulish nod.

"*Nein*, you're right," she continued, and stood straighter, if that were possible. "I'll go to Bethlehem instead! Tomorrow is Herr Goodstein's regular wagon train to Easton. Margaret and I will go with him."

"Absolutely not!" said Papa.

"Why not?" Mama asked.

"I need you here!"

"Why? You aren't wounded. John is."

"It's dangerous!"

47

"Herr Goodstein makes the trip safely every month."

"Anna, this is too much."

"*Nein*, Frederick. I just hope it's enough!"

II

Two days later, Bethlehem awoke to a return of the sticky heat that had characterized most of September in that year of 1777.

The Volpert women had spent their first evening in Bethlehem on an exhausting walking tour of town, after Herr Goodstein left them. Bethlehem's single inn had resolutely closed its doors against cramming even one more human body into its dangerously crowded quarters. When Margaret and her mother explained their mission, the innkeeper directed them to the Moravian Brethren's House. The religious community had relinquished their house to the American wounded. Perhaps they could help, he said.

"You can't come in tonight," the brother at the Brethren's House door had explained to a stubborn Mama. "In the morning we'll go over what lists we've been able to keep and see if your son is here."

"He is," she asserted.

"Yes," answered the man, with a doubtful, but kind look. "Anyway, it would be impossible to locate him tonight. And you and your daughter need to find lodging."

"We can stay with my son."

"Oh, no!" said the man, obviously taken aback. "There's no chance of that. The soldiers in there are rib to rib already."

He paused, gazing with sympathy at the weary women. "I'm sure our widows will be able to help you. In the morning, just ask for me, Brother Sebastian."

Early the next morning, after a restless night on the front parlor floor of the Widows' House, they watched Brother Sebastian run his finger methodically down column after column of names, all written in careless script on heavy paper.

"Kurtz . . . Hagen . . . White," he muttered as he read. "Roth . . . Meier . . . *oh!*"

Both Volperts brightened expectantly.

"Hm-m-m, no," he mumbled, shaking his big head while the women drooped.

"Wait!" he cried, and he jabbed his forefinger at one of the names. "Is this it?"

He held it out to Mama, but she only shook her head and nodded at her daughter, because she couldn't read. Margaret carefully spelled out the name, putting to use the reading lessons she'd coaxed from her brothers over the years.

"Mama!" she squealed, grabbing the older woman's arm with both hands. "That's John! He's here!"

"Naturally," said Mama calmly.

Finding John, however, was not so easy as finding his name. "Rib to rib" was no exaggeration. What Brother Sebastian failed to mention were the appalling conditions that came with the overcrowding, and the impossibility of keeping track of any individual patient. All they could do was search, bed by bed.

The hospital's first daunting impact was its smell. Even outside, Margaret and her mother were nearly overcome by the putrid odor of decaying flesh mixed with sulfur and smoke. In the muggy heat, the tightly shut windows held captive every awful subtlety of the stench.

"Why don't they air this place out?" Margaret whispered to her mother as they crossed the entrance hall on the ground floor. Brother Sebastian answered for her.

"The smoke purifies the air. We want to prevent what illness we can."

An undercurrent of sound swelled as they neared the first ward. When Brother Sebastian opened the heavy oak door, the awful noise of human suffering swept over them — men screaming at the top of their lungs, or jabbering in delirium, even weeping. Everywhere down the length of the room were men in pain or distress. Most lay on the floor with only straw for a mattress and rags for clothes. Many didn't even have a blanket to cover them. Immediately inside the room, one gaunt soldier sat up with an effort and stretched a thin arm out to Margaret.

"Give me something to drink, *Fräulein*, some rum, some whiskey," he whispered in American German. Then he lost his balance and fell over to one side. As he landed, he screamed, and Margaret cringed against her mother as she realized that his other arm was missing. Brother Sebastian quickly bent and turned the man onto his back again, gripping his hand and speaking soothingly to him. After a moment he rose and continued to guide the Volperts in their search.

"You must keep your eyes open and your wits about you," he cautioned. "It may be difficult to recognize your man."

The women passed one after another mangled and desperate soldier, all of them needing help, with only a handful of exhausted-looking Moravian sisters in evidence.

In the end, John spotted his mother and sister before they saw him.

"Mama," he called hoarsely, and immediately started to cough. Mama spun in the direction of his voice, then hurried over with Brother Sebastian and Margaret close behind.

"Well, there you are," she said sternly. "We have had a hard time finding you!"

"Mama," said John with a wan smile. "You are always yourself."

"*You*, however, are *not* yourself, I would say."

Then she lowered herself to the floor at his side, hugging him gently and probing him with anxious, maternal hands. A surgeon had closed his stomach wound, but as Mama examined it, she muttered angrily under her breath. John's long gash showed an unnatural, bloated red, and he labored over each rasping breath. His thick cough drew her frown.

"It's nothing," he said. "If I can just get out of this hell-hole, it'll go away. Hello, little Margaret," he added as he glimpsed her peering over their mother's shoulder.

"Oh Johnny," she began. "We thought we'd never find you. We thought . . ." She broke off on a high trembling note and bit her lip for control.

"We did *not* think," disputed her mother, sitting back on her heels. John reached past her to his sister. Margaret took his hand in both of hers and fell to her knees beside him, doing what her mother either would not or could not do,

51

laying her cheek against his and letting loose a sudden sea of tears in great, gulping sobs.

John put weak arms around his wailing sister, and she could hardly believe this frail young man was her "big" brother. She cried all the harder, but after a moment or two, felt herself taken firmly by the shoulders and pulled back from the invalid.

"Enough of that," Mama said briskly. "You'll make his shirt wet — if you can call that burnt rag a shirt."

Margaret and her mother spent that first day with John, in the vile corner that made his bed. Mama begged some clean straw and brought him the fresh clothes she'd carried with her from Reading, while Margaret followed her like a shadow.

The second morning, Margaret sat and watched her mother cluck and fuss over John for several hours. Meanwhile, all around her, young men lay alone, too sick even to help themselves to a drink of water. She turned her back and worked on the knitting she had brought, but their moans and cries for help through the long morning ate at her desperate concentration. Sometime around midday, a pair of Moravian sisters brought bowls of broth in for the men. They'd hardly begun to serve when a patient at the far end of the room let out a scream that lifted the hair on Margaret's scalp.

The sisters hurriedly laid down their trays and ran to him, calling for the doctor as they went. The minutes lengthened, the screaming continued — and the tray of bowls sat on the floor, out of reach of the men who awaited them.

"Get one of those for your brother," Mama said.

Margaret brought the soup, and settled down by John again. Irresistibly, though, her eyes traveled back to the bowls, then to the other men around them. She could still hear the turmoil at the end of the room. When would the sisters get back to serving?

Someone nearby called in quiet despair, "Sister!" and started to sob. Margaret looked at the knitting in her hands, and her vision blurred with sudden tears. She balled the work in a tangle of yarn and needles, not caring that she unraveled her last row, and laid it resolutely among her mother's supplies. Then she stood, cuffed her sleeves, and turned to the soup trays.

It took her more than an hour to serve and help feed the men. Then she carried water and medicine; she tore bandages from rags; she sponged fevered brows and wrists. And she listened. How badly these men, many of them German-Americans, had missed seeing and talking to people from outside their present nightmare world! Even the English-speaking soldiers were happy for Margaret's company, though she understood little of what they said. Just to see someone untouched by the war, to hear a young woman's sympathetic voice, brought a measure of healing. Their evident pleasure was Margaret's only bulwark against the nauseating sights and smells that filled her waking hours.

One day rolled over the next, and soon the bed on the Widows' House floor, the early morning and late evening walks through Bethlehem, and the grueling hospital work had all become a way of life. Mama gave every waking moment to John; every day found her looking more worn and worried. And Margaret left her short visits with John with a heavy heart.

III

Christian fought his way back to consciousness through air that choked him and noise that made his head throb. He opened his eyes, then squinted against the murky glare of the sky above him. Something wrong with that sky. Something wrong, too, with the ground beneath him. Everything jerked and swayed. Perhaps he should sleep awhile longer, till the craziness subsided.

"Help me! Please help me!" screamed a voice nearby. Christian's eyes shot open again. The cry turned into a long, wailing moan, and Christian made sense, at last, of the head-pounding noise around him — groaning men, rumbling wagon wheels, and the steady clip-clop of toiling horses' hooves — some kind of wagon train carried him along. But where?

The air was thick with dust and Christian began to cough. The spasm brought to life a multitude of sensations, each bad enough alone, but truly awful in combination. The worst was the pain that stabbed his thigh like a turning blade, shooting up and down the length of his leg and into his hip. He tried to roll, for some ease, only to discover a new agony. Every inch of his back pulsed with fiery awareness. He clutched compulsively, grabbed, and lifted a handful of straw. Something must be badly wrong with his back, that a bed of straw felt like live coals.

The earth jolted under him and he screamed again at the convulsion that seized his thigh. Slowly, he turned his head to one side. He found himself lying shoulder to shoulder with another man, someone he didn't recognize, who lay as still as death.

"Move those civilians along there, soldier! General Wayne's orders!" yelled a voice, hardly discernible through all the noise of the wagon wheels.

Christian's eyes flew open in alarm. With sudden clarity, his memory returned, jogged by the sound of authority in the command. But the tone of voice wasn't all he recognized. General Wayne! Another command filtered through the steady rumble and clatter. He didn't understand a word — but he knew it was an American and he knew he was in trouble.

The wagon lurched over a big rock in the road, and once more Christian was thrown violently from side to side. Clenching his jaw to keep from screaming, he squeezed his eyes shut and concentrated with all his strength on his memories.

He remembered Heinrich's going down, and he retraced his own steps up the slippery bank and into chaos. He saw again the young American who had charged him like a madman, misstepping into the blade of Christian's outstretched bayonet at the last moment — the wounded soldier's stare, his glazing eyes, his limp drop.

Then had come the blinding flash and searing in Christian's leg.

"Who won?" Christian asked aloud. Then, in rapid succession, "Who cares?" He was a wounded prisoner. Who knew what the rebels would do to him once they discovered him to be a Hessian soldier. Christian's head throbbed with every jostle of his mobile bed. The thoughts began to blur and swirl in his darkening consciousness, and then he was plunging his bayonet mercilessly into the stomach of his enemy. The man's face came round slowly, and Christian stabbed, and stabbed again. Still the eyes stared with innocence. Christian filled his lungs with one consuming gasp and screamed, hiding in the only refuge he could think of, the cave behind his own eyelids. His victim grabbed his shoulders and shook him, yelling "Wake up! Wake up!" in a strange high voice. Christian cried "No!" through clenched teeth, but the shaking continued.

Finally, his resistance broke, and he gazed once again into the innocent, accusing eyes. Then he blinked in surprise. Because, although the eyes were there, the identical piercing blue between heavy gold fringe, the face had changed. Instead of the American soldier — that Hessian-killer with his blaming eyes — Christian stared into the alarmed face of a young woman who sat at his side with her hand on his shoulder. She was pale as new snow, striking in her fairness, the hollows under her familiar eyes dark like evening shadows.

"Oh finally!" she cried, slumping forward slightly. "Thank God!"

Then she covered her face with her hands and began to sob.

Christian shielded his eyes with his hand, trying to make sense of this new dream. The girl's weeping turned into a series of hiccups and sniffs while other sounds swelled — a

56

hoarse cry, moans, muted conversation, and a distant clatter like dishes.

"Here now! Margaret! What's this about?" demanded a man's voice suddenly. Christian looked up in surprise. He saw a pair of muddy shoes and splattered stockings, black coarsely woven breeches, and a soiled linen waistcoat whose bone buttons strained the cloth over a broad belly — all this topped by a face that peered down at Christian, a round, jowly face meant for a jovial man.

"What have you done to her!" he cried, as blotchy red seeped up his neck.

"Oh Doctor," began the young woman called Margaret, scrubbing at her eyes with her apron. Christian listened in surprise to their oddly phrased German.

"You haven't the decency you were born with!" exclaimed the physician. As he spoke, he shoved Christian's good leg to one side with his foot, at the same time taking Margaret's elbows and raising her to her knees. "There, there," he said, patting her awkwardly while he glared at the injured man.

"Please stop!" cried Margaret and pulled away. "He didn't do anything!"

The doctor's bushy eyebrows shot up, then plunged to form a *V* above his nose.

"Then why the blazes are you crying?" he demanded. He straightened and scowled at the pair.

Christian turned his wary gaze from the doctor to the young woman. She looked disheveled, as though she'd just been in a fight. In fact, one white cheek had a discolored lump just showing under her tangled hair.

"I . . . I don't know," she answered and pushed her

hair back from her face. "I'm just tired. I've tended this man all night. He's been awfully sick."

"So is everyone else here, girl!" exclaimed the doctor. "And every other one of them would be more worth your attention!"

"What do you mean?" Margaret asked with a frown. "He had no one to care for him! He needed help. Why shouldn't I help him?"

"Because he's a Hessian," said an ironic voice. She turned to the soldier behind her, who was lying on his side with his head propped up on one hand. *They know!* thought Christian. *But why am I here?* Then a new disturbance distracted the group.

"Bring them in here," bellowed a deep voice from the next room. A huge man in Continental uniform strode heavily past the open door, making the floor shake. Behind him came pairs of tattered, begrimed soldiers carrying makeshift stretchers between them. On each pallet lay a body, but only one of the victims showed signs of life, clinging pitifully to the poles of his stretcher and screaming out in pain.

"What's this now?" the physician asked. "We've no room here. What do they think they're doing?"

The doctor marched stoutly out of the room, muttering and gesturing all the way.

In the corner, Margaret helped Christian to sit up. She sat beside him on the floor, studiously picking pieces of straw from her skirt while he concentrated on keeping his balance. After a short, awkward pause, Margaret broke the silence.

"Are you really?" she asked shyly.

"Really what?" replied Christian. They still didn't look at each other.

"One of them," she answered. "A Hessian?"

"Yes," he said quietly, "a private in General Knyphausen's Jäger corps."

As his balance returned, he opened the rip in his filthy breeches over the wound in his leg. Not pretty, but he'd seen far worse.

"Oh," said Margaret. Another lengthy silence, then, "Well, I must go and find my mama."

"Wait!" said Christian with sudden urgency. At last he looked directly at his nurse. He could feel his face heating up, but he plowed on. "I . . . I want to thank you. I think it must have been hard for you, and maybe no one else would have done it. So . . . so, thank you."

"I didn't do much," she said, and she glanced at him quickly before resuming her inspection of her apron. A strange expression worked at her face, but all she said was, "I'm glad you're better."

"Did I do that to you?" Christian blurted suddenly.

"What?"

Christian reached his hand out toward Margaret's cheek, almost touching it, while she sat transfixed like a frightened animal.

"You have a bruise on your cheek," he explained and let his hand drop. "Did I do that?"

Margaret felt the spot and winced. Christian winced in sympathy. Then, by some magic of the moment, they smiled at one another.

"I suppose you did," she said. "But it doesn't hurt much. When were *you* hurt?"

Christian told her, all the while puzzling over her vague

familiarity. Did she remind him of the German girls he'd grown up with?

"Oh! My brother was wounded there! He's here now, too. He's not doing so well, though." Margaret's bright eyes clouded over.

"I'm sorry," Christian said, then quickly added, "but I'm sure it helps him to have you here."

"I hardly have a chance to see him," she confided in a low voice. "Mama insists on doing everything for him. It's all right, though," she added hastily, "I've had such a lot to do. They haven't much help for all these poor men."

"*Nein*," agreed Christian, scanning the full room. "I can see that."

They lapsed once more into silence, only this time it felt comfortable to be quiet. No one seemed to notice them in their dim corner. A pair of Moravian women had come in with bowls of thin gruel for breakfast, while a few of the stronger invalids talked among themselves.

"Why did you come to America?" asked Margaret.

Christian considered the question in surprise.

"I came because I was sent," he said with a slight frown.

"But we have nothing against your country," said Margaret. "My parents even grew up in Germany. My brother John was born there. Why do you want to fight us?"

"You Americans cannot disobey your king and think he will do nothing about it," answered Christian. "We must know our place, and do our duty to our superiors."

As he spoke, Christian could feel a fine film of sweat forming on his face. Margaret's brows had drawn low over her eyes and her mouth seemed set in dissatisfaction. But when Christian wiped a hand across his upper lip, she was suddenly transformed.

"I think you should lie down, now," she said briskly. She helped him lower himself to his back, all maidenly reserve momentarily forgotten. Then she began to rise. "You need some real sleep, now that your fever is gone."

"Please stay a moment more," he said. "Tell me who you are."

Margaret gazed at Christian out of those intense eyes, shadowed as they were by the bruise and weariness. She sat again slowly, straightening her skirt around her and folding her hands in her lap. She spoke, then, in a gentle storyteller's cadence, of a place called Reading, and of her family. Her face changed as she described her parents, her brothers, and her young sister, but always she smiled. When she had exhausted her small repertoire of anecdotes, she said, "Now it's your turn."

Christian tried, haltingly, to match her easy style, but he could tell Margaret struggled with some of what he said. At one point she perked up considerably.

"Are you really a cobbler?" she asked, wide-eyed.

"At home I am, *ja*."

"Well, so is my father! And my brother John, too. At least, he was until the war."

As she mentioned her brother, Margaret seemed startled.

"I must go," she said, as she started to her feet, her eyes lowered. At the same time, one of the women serving the gruel approached her.

"Your mama is here, child," she said as she knelt beside one of her patients. "Perhaps you should find her, and then go for some sleep, *ja?*"

Before Margaret could reply, another voice interrupted, the rude, rough voice of an invalid several men down the line.

"I said, YOU; Hessian pig!"

A convalescent sat propped against a rough post nearby, staring past Margaret at Christian with a nasty expression.

"I beg your pardon?" said Christian in a low voice.

"I asked you what you thought about Bennington," the man said in American-German. He spoke loudly, as though he thought Christian might be hard of hearing.

"I don't know Bennington," Christian responded. "Is he an American officer?"

A burst of laughter broke out among several of the angry man's friends.

"It's a place," murmured Margaret.

"You know about Bennington, Vermont, don't you, Hessian?" he continued. "Where our hunters put you professionals in the ground?"

His comrades stirred in gratified assent, while the Moravian sister whispered to Margaret, "You'd better go, dear." Margaret didn't budge.

"And what about Paoli, king's boy?" asked the man.

"Is Paoli a place, too?" asked Christian thickly.

"We lost it," answered Christian's tormentor with a growling ferocity. "But we fought with honor. Unlike you, PIG, and those Redcoat cowards."

"We fight with honor," said Christian flatly. "German soldiers are trained to be honorable soldiers."

"Honorable like snakes," said the man and he spat. Christian felt Margaret recoil, as he himself tensed for action. The American continued. "You didn't stop with the battle. Never that. We've heard about the 'prisoners' you took. The prisoners who mysteriously never made it to a prison!"

"What do you mean?" cried Christian. "Certainly they did!"

"Only as corpses," said the man, almost hissing. Margaret turned a full, wide-eyed gaze on Christian. Other men in the room called out.

"And what about the families you murdered in their homes?" said one.

"We never did!" Christian shouted. "It's the Americans who do such things! We are *soldiers*, in the Jäger corps, not butchers!"

"Liar!" screamed the man who had started the commotion. He tried to push himself to his feet as though to lunge for Christian. Christian, too, tried to rise. But Margaret pushed him firmly down again, as she herself jumped up.

"Stop it!" she yelled over the growing clamor. She stood between American and Hessian, trembling, with her hands on her hips, her hair in a wild jumble around her deathly white face. "Sit down!" she ordered the half-risen accuser.

The soldier stared at her, his mouth open. Then slowly, he lowered himself onto his pile of straw. Christian started to speak, but she whirled around to face him with the same strength of purpose she had shown toward his persecutor.

"Hush!" she commanded. "Just don't say another word!"

As she spoke, Christian could see the uncertainty in her eyes. About the truth of the accusations? Or about what she was doing?

"What now?" demanded the doctor from the doorway, his voice irritable. "This room is the only one giving us trouble!"

He stood, arms akimbo, with his fat belly protruding, and frowned so hard that his face seemed ready to close in on itself. Crowding in at the door behind him were the sisters who had run to fetch him when the dialogue turned mean, an enormous Moravian, and an older woman. When she saw Margaret, planted like an armed guard in front of Christian, the woman pushed peremptorily into the room.

"Margaret," she declared. "It's time to go."

"But Mama," Margaret began. She never finished. The soldiers had found her intimidating in her passion, but this woman did not. She was taken firmly by the arm and led out, with no time to think or argue. The angry Americans, meanwhile, had shot their bolt. Aside from a few hostile glances, Christian found himself ignored, with only his memories of his young nurse for comfort or company.

Chapter Four

I

"Margaret," Mama said. "I think it is time to go home."

"But, what about John?" cried Margaret. "How will he do without you?"

"We've done all we can for now, child. He's just too weak to travel yet."

"Perhaps soon, though," interjected Brother Sebastian. The three stood together at the front entrance of the Brethren's House.

Margaret's head swam with weariness and sudden overpowering dismay.

"Mama, please, consider —" she said.

"That's enough, Margaret," said her mother as she led her out into the street.

Later that day, after packing and a short rest, Margaret and her mother returned to the hospital to spend their short remaining time with John.

"I'll miss you, Margaret," he said, while Mama spoke to Brother Sebastian with some final instructions. "I wish I were going with you."

Margaret stared down into his worn face. The color was all wrong, gray and chalky, his skin like thin paper.

"You'll come home soon," she said.

"Mama says you've been nursing the enemy," he said with a smile.

"He didn't *seem* like the enemy, Johnny," she answered, seeing the Hessian's face again in her imagination.

"I know!" he answered. "I thought that too! Strange, isn't it, when the enemy becomes real people who look as though they ought to live in Reading? What'll happen to him, do you think?"

"Brother Sebastian told me they'd send him to a prisoners' camp within the month, since he's nearly well," Margaret said and chewed on her lip pensively.

"You don't look as though you think much of that idea," said her brother.

"He's a prisoner," she said solemnly. "Where else would he go?"

"Don't worry too much about the Hessian," John said softly, ignoring her half-hearted denial. "Many of them are put to work and don't have to live in the prison camps at all. Some of them even come over to our side."

Farewells sadly completed, early the next morning the Volpert women headed homeward, once more with the Goodstein party. Their forced cheerfulness at John's bedside was abandoned and they rode immersed in all the worried sorrow they'd tried to hide from John.

Margaret paid scant attention to the others. She was lost in her own world — not the childhood world she had left in Reading. This present world was real, full of suffering, tragedy, rage, and confusion — all terribly new to her. Was this growing up, carrying these painful impressions from the hospital? If so, growing up cost a great deal. She had crossed a bridge only to have it destroyed behind her.

Yet, amid all the gloom, Margaret's mind came back, almost guiltily, to Christian Molitor. She went over their short conversation many times in her mind, and remembered, too, the accusations leveled at him by the Americans. Then she thought of his being sent, half-well, to a prison camp. As she rode home alongside her mother and Herr Goodstein, she swayed and bobbed with them to the wagon's motion, matching their stolid silence — and surpassing it.

II

The air tingled with change. Or so it seemed to Margaret as the Goodstein party rolled into Reading, two days after quitting Bethlehem. The smell of change seemed to blow with the autumn wind across the Schuylkill River. Certainly, summer had passed while they were gone, lost for another year. But the seasons' change had never left Margaret with such an uneasy feeling before. She sat on the edge of her wagon seat as they rattled down the lane, as though someone had called to her suddenly, "Watch out!"

The Goodstein wagon bumped to a halt by the Volperts' front gate.

"Ah, at last," said Mama with a sigh, patting Margaret's

knee in satisfaction. The two travelers climbed down stiffly, then accepted their baggage from a weary Herr Goodstein. While Mama handled thanks and payment, Margaret walked slowly up the path to the front door. The door was shut tight against the cool evening, the whitewash glowing clean and bright, especially in the dusk. Where were her father and sister, she wondered.

No sooner had the thought crossed her mind, than the door was flung wide and they erupted, the tiny remnant of the clan who had minded the home fires and shod the limping army while the rest ventured abroad.

"Margaret!" squealed Charlotte. She threw herself against her sister's travel-soiled skirt and hugged tightly. Margaret dropped her bag and stooped to kiss one rosy cheek. As she did, Charlotte wriggled away to her mother.

"Did you see the Redcoats? Where's John? Does he have a scar? What's Bethlehem like? Were you attacked? Why couldn't I come?"

Mama smothered the tumble of questions in her chuckling embrace, ignoring the deluge. Papa, meanwhile, herded family and baggage inside.

Everything was orderly, all in place down to the last candlewick. Firelight spilled through the kitchen doorway, forming a warm yellow pool on the scrubbed plank floor; and the unmistakable aroma of sausage hung in the air like a savory mist. Mama stopped abruptly at the front door, surveying the tidiness with surprise, then returned to fussing over Charlotte like a goose with her gosling.

Papa put his arm around Margaret and squeezed.

"Welcome home, little one," he said with quiet affection.

Behind the gentle welcome in his eyes hovered the silent question, *Where is John?*

"He's still too sick to travel," Margaret answered before he could ask. "But he seemed better after Mama's nursing."

Her father nodded as they followed Mama into the kitchen. All traces of the evening meal had already been wiped away.

"Papa, how have you managed so well?" Margaret whispered. "I didn't realize you were such a good housekeeper."

"Two people make little mess," he said. "When our boys are home . . ."

Papa moved to the hearth and, squinting and grimacing with each thrust of the poker, he stirred up the coals till flames licked and crackled at the wood. Margaret hung up her cloak with a sigh and helped herself to some rusks from a basket on the bread rack and a chunk of her mother's sweet goat cheese.

"To bed," Mama was saying to her clinging child.

"But Mama," moaned Charlotte, with a pout. "It's only just dark, and you haven't told us anything!"

She flung herself over to the fire where Margaret was settling with her food.

"Um-m-m," the little girl sighed. "I love rusks. Can I have one?" She folded her plump hands in front of her and smiled so hopefully that Margaret couldn't help chuckling. It seemed a long time since Margaret had seen anything as simple as Charlotte's round-eyed greed.

"Come now," said Mama with determination. "I will tell you all about it while I put you to bed."

"Wait," Papa said from the hearth. Margaret focused on

his face with difficulty in the firelight. She recognized that tight-skinned look around his eyes and mouth. She had seen it on John himself when they kissed him *auf Wiedersehen*. When Papa spoke again, he had only one question.

"When can he come home?"

His wife's answer — "I don't know" — told the hard, straight truth at last.

After Charlotte had finally been coaxed to bed, Margaret sat with her parents by the fire. Papa had heard news of Jacob while they were gone. He'd fought at Paoli with General Wayne, fought so well that he was honored as a hero.

"He is like my father," Papa said. "He fights with his Prussian blood."

Not until the moon was high and the fire low that night did they make their yawning way to bed. And only after Margaret had climbed between her down quilts did her earlier sense of encroaching change come flooding back. Then, in the privacy of her own thoughts, she saw again the endless fields of hospital tents arrayed in every available space around the Brethren's House in Bethlehem. She remembered the Widows' House and the tiny room, hardly a cupboard, that had been her only home for weeks. Lying safe in the deep warmth of her parents' house, she could hardly believe in the stinking, crowded hospital, with its hundreds of men, wounded and sick, laid out in rows on their dirty straw, like pieces of raw meat at a late autumn slaughter.

Change *was* in the air. And as surely as she knew a transformation had taken hold of her, Margaret knew she hadn't seen its end.

III

Late the following evening, Margaret laid aside her needlework and rose from her fireside chair.

"Papa is late at his work," she commented to her mother. Mama bent low over the mending in her lap.

"As always," she said around the pin she held between her teeth. "Your papa has been late in his shop nearly every night since the war began. And he probably will be until it ends."

Margaret fiddled with the back of her chair, chewing her lower lip.

"Do you suppose he's thirsty?" she asked. "Maybe I should take him some ale."

Still squinting, Mama looked up from her work, the deeper lines around her eyes and mouth accentuated in the shadowy room.

"That's a good idea, Margaret," she said. "Take some of the strudel as well."

"*Ja*, certainly."

Moments later Margaret was out the kitchen door and into the yard with full hands. She crossed quickly in the chilly evening breeze to the work shed with its dusty window glowing.

While she balanced the full mug in one hand, the plate of strudel in the other, Margaret lifted the door latch with her elbow and pushed the door open with her foot. The door scraped against the hard floor as she pushed it. Inside, she heard her father's voice before she saw him.

"John?" he asked in an odd thick mumble. "Is that you, son?" Margaret shivered.

"No, Papa, it's Margaret," she said and came the rest of the way in.

Papa sat hunched over his workbench, running his hands through his hair. The skin on one side of his face wore the pattern of his rough sleeve and his eyes were dark and red-rimmed. For the first time, Margaret noticed the new gray in his hair, the furrows and crevices that sketched his cheeks and brow. If Margaret had passed into adulthood in the last several weeks, her father had moved to the very edge of old age. He ran a hand down his drawn face and pinched the bridge of his nose between thumb and forefinger.

"Margaret," he said in something closer to his normal voice. "Yes, child, what is it?"

"I brought you some ale, Papa," she said, stepping up to his bench, looking carefully away from his face, staring at the tools, the leather, a boot.

She pushed his work aside with the edge of the mug and set it down. Then, in a sudden flood of passion, she threw her arms around him and sobbed.

"Hush," he said softly. "Everything will be all right, you'll see."

Margaret cried on her father's shoulder as she had on John's, only now no Mama pulled her away. She knelt beside her father while he held her head against his chest and stroked it in a quieting motion. When at last she moved away and looked at him squarely, he seemed once more the father she knew and depended on. He raised the mug to his lips and took a sip, followed by a full swallow.

"Thank you," he said with a smile. "This tastes wonderful." He took another long drink, then noticed the strudel. "And what's that?"

"Mama thought you might be hungry, too," she answered. She passed him the plate that looked more fragile in his large, hard hands. Papa tasted the pastry and sighed, looking more himself with every passing bite.

"Well, I thank your mama, too, then," he said. Margaret sat silently, watching him eat, so silently and for so long that he finally stopped and looked at her. He said, "I can bring the dishes in when I'm through, if you'd like to go."

"That's all right," she said. "I'll wait."

One of Papa's eyebrows twitched and his eyes widened slightly, but he only nodded in reply. His eating slowed. He seemed quite recovered now, and Margaret stirred, straightening her apron and clearing her throat.

"Papa," she said and paused.

"*Ja*, Margaret," prompted her father. Margaret pleated and unpleated one edge of her apron, staring at it while she framed her day's thoughts into careful words.

"You're awfully busy, aren't you?" she said at last, still not looking at him.

"*Ja*," he said. He laid down his fork and folded his hands on the bench.

"It must be terribly hard for you to do without John and

73

Jacob," she continued, steadily folding and refolding the apron all the while.

"It is hard, *ja.*"

"It would be good, wouldn't it, if you could get some other help?"

"Good indeed!" exclaimed Frederick. "Miraculous!"

"I might know where you could," she said slowly, giving her apron a light tug and smoothing the wrinkles she had just made.

"You do?" Frederick replied with a smile. "And where is that? *You* aren't thinking of taking up the trade, are you?"

"What? Me?" said Margaret, surprised at last into meeting her father's gaze. She laughed suddenly. "Of course not!"

"What then?" he asked. "Surely not the Scheffer boy! His father swears he has ten thumbs."

"Oh no! Never him!" she cried.

"Well?" queried her father.

"Well," she returned. She stared at him for a moment. Then she took a deep breath and plunged ahead. "Papa, I met this soldier at the hospital. I mean, I helped take care of him. Anyway, I found out that he's a cobbler, just like you. And he's nearly well, too. He could leave the hospital almost anytime. I thought . . . well, maybe . . ."

"That he could come and work here?" her father finished for her.

"Yes," she agreed, her hands knotted together tensely in her lap.

"But surely he has his own home, his own shop to tend when he's well. Or perhaps he'll go back to fight."

"Oh." Margaret's gaze dropped once again to her lap.

"Well, to tell the truth, Papa, *nein*. He hasn't a home and he's through fighting."

"No home?" asked her father in surprise.

"Not in the colonies," she answered.

"Where then?"

"In Germany."

"Germany? How is that?" he asked. Margaret looked up once more.

"He's a Hessian prisoner, Papa," she said. "He was taken to the hospital by mistake and now they want to get rid of him, to send him to a prison camp."

"A Hessian," said Papa. He was silent for some time.

Margaret sat absolutely still now, watching every nuance of expression on her father's face, and she waited. She hardly breathed.

"Your mama says the hospital is bad," he said at last. "And that John needs to come home."

"It is not a place for getting well," she agreed.

"I have been thinking today that perhaps I should go and fetch him," he said. "I could take a shipment of supplies for the army at the same time."

"Oh, Papa! How wonderful that would be!" cried Margaret. "And all the soldiers need so much more than they have."

"I wouldn't be sorry to bring back some help at the same time," he mused and caught his daughter's wide-eyed stare. His mouth made a slow smile to match the growing twinkle in his eyes, and Margaret jumped to her feet with an answering grin.

"I'll take these things in for you," she said and whisked

75

her father's half-full mug and plate from under his nose, turning and hurrying to the door.

"Margaret," he called. She stopped and looked back. Her father's smile broadened, but his words were serious. "You will, perhaps, not mention this matter to your mama?"

Margaret nodded wisely, then left the shop. She would happily leave the subject of the Hessian to Papa.

"Absolutely not!" stormed her mother the next morning, when Papa told her what he meant to do. "Never!"

"Mama, he'd be working for our side," pleaded Margaret. Her father threw her a warning glance.

"He's one of *them!*" Mama cried. "Murderers!"

"I need the help badly," said her husband. "It makes more sense to use the prisoners to produce what our army needs than to leave them in prisons where they can only use it up."

"Let someone else take him in," argued his wife. "I won't have him in my home, not on any account."

"Anna, messages have been sent all over the colonies about the Hessians," Papa continued. "The Continental Congress has asked us to befriend them, if we can. Many of the Hessians have already deserted. They work or fight for us now, because of the kindness shown them in this country."

"I won't! Don't ask me . . ."

"Anna," he interrupted. Mama matched him stare for stare. Then, as the moment lengthened, her gaze dropped.

"Well, I won't feed him!" she declared and stomped out of the room.

Throughout the remainder of the day, an uneasy truce

reigned, and through the days that followed, as well. A stubbornly frigid truce between husband and wife, it spilled over onto their daughters and made their home a place of tiptoes and frowns.

By the end of the week, everyone was relieved when Papa announced his imminent departure for Bethlehem. Margaret gave him Brother Sebastian's name, and a careful description of the Hessian and his whereabouts in the hospital.

The morning Papa left, Margaret and Charlotte stood together in the early mist as their father mounted the wagon seat. Each daughter sent a message to John, and Margaret handed Papa a package of food her mother had prepared for him.

Only at the last possible moment did Mama appear, carrying her travel bag. She lifted it to her husband without expression.

"Some clothes and a blanket for John's ride home," she explained flatly.

Papa stowed the bag at his feet wordlessly. Then he turned and surveyed his family. He sighed deeply.

"Anna," he said.

As they stared at one another, the hard set of her mouth softened.

"Be careful," she said.

"*Ja*," he replied. "And you."

With that, he nodded, smiled, and waved at his children, and slapped the reins against his horse's flank. As he moved off, Margaret prayed for him, for her brother — and for the Hessian, who would soon join the Volpert household.

IV

Christian's last day at the Moravian hospital began like every other of the previous weeks, with a slow, careful tour of the campgrounds outside. Once his fever had broken, Christian grew steadily stronger, his wound and burns far less painful than his alien presence among these American rebels. Breathing fresh air, seeing different faces, and exercising his weak limbs were heady medicine for someone inactive for so long.

Brother Sebastian found him just heading back in for breakfast. A stranger strode beside the Moravian, wearing the grim look of shock that betrayed every visitor.

"This is Herr Frederick Volpert," said Brother Sebastian. "He has a proposition for you."

Herr Volpert greeted Christian with more civility than the Hessian was used to receiving. He explained that if Christian would agree to work in his cobbler shop and promise to remain with him until the end of the war, then prison camp would not be necessary.

Christian had chewed over such a decision many times with his Jäger friends. Now the choice seemed easy.

"I'd be grateful, sir," he said.

"He has nothing to wear," Brother Sebastian said.

"I have clothes to give him," Herr Volpert answered. "I carried little extra for myself, but I have my son's."

"I suppose they'll fit?"

Both men turned to scrutinize Christian's appearance. He, meanwhile, stared at the tents beyond them, plucking at his hospital rags.

"The clothes will do. My son is much larger through the shoulders, but the height is about the same," said Herr Volpert, and for a moment, his eyes seemed to lose focus. "They wouldn't fit John anyway. He's half his own size, now."

So it was decided that Christian would leave Bethlehem in John's clothes, in the company of John's father, to live in John's house. It only remained for Herr Volpert to make his final farewell to John himself.

For as long as he lived, Christian would never forget that meeting. John was lying on his side, his back to the room. When Herr Volpert called him, he rolled over cautiously, holding his stomach. In that slow revelation of his face, Christian's recurring nightmare came to life. His sense of balance deserted him, and he closed his eyes defensively. But there was no waking from this dream. When Christian looked again, John lay there still.

John greeted Christian with an inattentive courtesy, giving no evidence that he recognized his battle assailant, or even the clothes. He was too taken up with being left again to the mercies of the overworked hospital staff, and deprived as well of sight and sound of his family. Christian stood to one side in helpless silence as father and son said goodbye.

"Son, I want to bring you home with me," said Herr Volpert, frowning deeply.

"I think I wouldn't make it, Papa," John answered in a voice thinned by pain. "Maybe in a week or two. If I could just be rid of this infernal flux, I might get my strength back."

He interrupted himself with a rattling cough, and his father lowered his head, shaking it and sighing.

"How can I leave you in this place?" Herr Volpert asked, casting a look of disgust over the foul-smelling room.

"I don't want you to!" John replied. He smiled and reached out for his father's hand. "But I think I'd better wait." His face was suddenly serious. "I don't want to die, Papa."

"You won't die, son," Herr Volpert said quietly. "I can't stay now, but I'll be back. And you'll come home with me then, I promise!"

John stared at his father, a pale glimmer of hope in his fever-dulled eyes, while the older man talked on, holding his son's hand all the while — remembering better days they had shared in Reading, planning grandly for John's future in the family trade, discussing the bad news of Howe's occupation of Philadelphia, and the good news of the British surrender of Fort Ticonderoga in New York.

Christian tried not to listen. He tried to blend into the background. When the farewell finally came to an end, and Christian left the second floor for the last time, his relief was almost boundless.

Once on the road, Herr Volpert drove in grim silence, leaving Christian alone to his own emotions. They continued in this way until day's end, when they stopped at a roadside tavern.

The next morning, they ate watered-down gruel that didn't tempt them to linger, then made their way onward with the rising sun warming their backs, thankful for another fair day.

They spoke little, as one milestone followed another. But Herr Volpert exhibited none of the hostility Christian had come to expect in the hospital, and the day was uncommonly fine. By the time the wagon slowed to a halt in the Volperts' shed yard, the sun and the distance from the hospital had warmed Christian through.

"This is it," said Herr Volpert. "Home."

The first one to notice their arrival was a young girl just leaving one of the outbuildings.

"Charlotte," Herr Volpert said in Christian's ear. "My youngest."

Charlotte leaped like a goat over a neat stack of pumpkins piled beside the back corner of the house, her ankle-length skirt held high. Then she galloped to the wagon with a whoop, only to come to a sliding standstill at the sight of the Hessian. She stood round-eyed with curiosity as Christian and her father climbed down off the wagon's seat.

The door at the side of the house opened wide, then, and a woman rushed out with someone close on her heels. Christian's body tensed and his head swam at the sight of them — he had seen these two before! In the fading light, the woman must not have known him until she practically had her arms around his neck. When she saw his face, inches from her own, she jerked back. She stared frantically in every direction, looking in the wagon, around the yard, even skyward. Then she whirled on her husband.

"*Get him out of those clothes!*" she spat, pointing at Christian as though she were aiming a gun. Then she turned on her heel and marched back into the house, leaving her family staring after her open-mouthed.

Finally, Christian found himself face to face with the ministering angel who had nursed him and defended him in the hospital. Margaret stood speechless in the wake of her mother's rage, looking first at Christian, then at Herr Volpert. Hopelessly uncertain, Christian turned his back on them all, moving to the horse that had pulled him here and stroking her flank again and again with shaking hands.

Chapter Five

The Volperts stood in silence, assembled at one end of the long table in the kitchen, heads bowed for prayer. The morning fire had yet to burn off the night's damp chill. Even so, the snap and hiss of burning wood was an antidote to the driving October rain that threw itself, like handfuls of pebbles, against the windowpanes. Christian stood with the Volpert family and watched.

From the table's head, Herr Volpert offered thanks and called down mercy on his soldier sons and the country they served away from home. To his right, Frau Volpert stood in rigid concentration, with her arms folded tightly against her midriff. While her husband prayed on, she moved her lips silently, as though adding petitions of her own.

Across the table from Frau Volpert stood her girls: Charlotte, rocking from foot to foot, bumping into Margaret's skirt with each sway; and Margaret, remarkably still, hands folded before her.

Christian watched each one in turn, but his gaze always returned to Frau Volpert. In her rage of the previous evening, she had refused to serve him dinner with the family and exiled him for the night to the loft over her husband's shop. There, Christian had perched on the edge of his narrow wood-frame bed and made a table of the washstand for the cold supper Herr Volpert contrived. This would be Christian's room, Herr Volpert had explained. But in the future, Christian could expect to eat in the house. The upset was just shock, he said. His wife would be herself come morning. So Christian had settled himself under the steeply sloping ceiling, dozing in fits and starts, and waiting out the dark.

In the morning, Herr Volpert fetched him for breakfast, true to his word. The others already stood at the table when the men came in. Charlotte curtsied and giggled as her father introduced her. Margaret lowered her eyes and offered a quiet *"guten Morgen,"* while Frau Volpert said nothing, only stared straight ahead with half-closed eyes.

Now, a solemn "amen" brought the tableau to life and the breakfast ritual began. Herr Volpert served helpings of fried corn mush and sausage with apples from large porringers, then passed them around. The pitcher of molasses followed, and cups of green tea. Christian ate the sticky-sweet mush without tasting it. The clack of cutlery, the crackle and spit of the fire, and the steady drumming of the rain were the sole conversation.

As he ate, Christian noticed glances thrown his way. Charlotte stared at his hair, tied in a tight queue at the nape of his neck. He knew from watching his Hessian comrades that it bobbed with every motion of his head, and he tried not to move. Margaret, too, peered regularly at Christian, looking quickly away if ever he caught her eye. How different she seemed now, straight and proper at the table with her family, so different from the tousled nurse who had sat by his side on the floor.

When the last platter had finally been scraped clean, Frau Volpert broke the long silence, directing Margaret in the cleaning-up. The women rose and began clearing while Charlotte hopped off to her corncob dolls by the hearth. Herr Volpert cast a doubtful eye at Christian in John's brown homespun clothes.

"You'll need more than what you've got on to keep warm in the shop today," he mused. "Especially for your legs. Wait here and I'll look among the boys' things for some thicker stockings and a heavy jacket."

Christian stood awkwardly while Herr Volpert trudged up the narrow stairs. Frau Volpert kept her back to Christian, filling the kitchen with the clatter of dishware and orders to Margaret. He stared at Margaret's fair hair, hanging nearly to her waist from the blue ribbon that held it away from her face. She hadn't done more than greet him since he arrived. Incredible, he thought, that she was not only his nurse, but sister to the soldier he'd fought and injured. A dull ache took hold of Christian's throat as memories pressed in, and he looked away quickly.

Meanwhile, Charlotte had abandoned her corncob children for a box of the boys' marbles. Christian watched her noisy rummaging in the box, now, with growing fascination.

The little girl's blond chubbiness reminded him of the baby sister he'd left a year and a half ago in Germany, as did her pout of concentration. Suddenly, a grin of satisfaction broke across her face, as she pulled out a knotted loop of yarn. After a moment's consideration, she placed the yarn on the floor practically at Christian's feet, carefully shaping it into an approximate circle. Then she moved a short distance away, squatted down, and reached into the box for a marble. This she rolled toward the yarn, but it overshot and came to rest against Christian's shoe. She repeated the process and missed again.

Christian couldn't resist. He squatted in an imitation of the child's posture, grabbed one of the marbles and rolled it back to Charlotte's feet. She looked up with a giggle and shot again. Again Christian returned her marble, aiming it exactly between her scuffed shoe tops. This continued, the pace picking up with each roll, until Charlotte's mounting excitement got the better of her. She laughed out loud, and clapped.

"Watch this!" she crowed. Then she filled both her fists with marbles and flung them higgledy-piggledy in Christian's direction. Forgetting himself — and the others in the room — Christian gave a hoot of answering pleasure.

At that, Frau Volpert spun around in alarm, then flew across the room to her youngest child, grabbed her by the arm and pulled her abruptly to her feet.

"That's enough!" she yelled. "Just look at what you've done!" She gave Charlotte a small shake as she pointed at the scattered marbles, ignoring Christian entirely.

At the same time, Herr Volpert reappeared at the foot of the stairs with a bundle of garments.

"Here now," he said with eyebrows raised high. "What's all this?"

Frau Volpert glared wordlessly at nothing in particular, while her husband crossed the room to her side, kicking the scattered marbles out of the way as he came. Charlotte, in the meantime, had recovered from the initial shock of her mother's descent. Now, her face crumpled and she started to bawl at the top of her healthy lungs.

Christian stood wretchedly alone.

Herr Volpert sighed and shook his head, running his hand through his hair, then scratching briefly at his neck.

"Here we go, Christian," he said, handing over the clothes. "Just bring these along. It's time to get to work."

With that, he led the way out of the kitchen. But before Christian closed the door behind them, he saw Frau Volpert bend swiftly and bundle her wailing child into her arms.

Herr Volpert had just crossed the puddled shed yard to the shop when the front gate squeaked open and a short, round man wearing an undersized beaver hat waddled through.

"Frederick!" he called over the rain's loud drumming. As he raised one hand in greeting, he swung his other up and Christian saw that he carried a boot. "Glad to see you're back on the job! *Wilkommen in der Heimat,* John."

"Not John," said Herr Volpert. "Christian. I've hired him on. This is Herr Scheffer, Christian," he added quietly.

Christian drew the man's second glance, but no further comment.

"Good to see you, Carl," Herr Volpert continued, and he ushered his customer in ahead of Christian. "Give me a moment, if you will, to get the boy going, then I'll see what you have there."

Carl Scheffer waved him on complacently and moved to the small iron stove Christian had earlier stirred to warmth.

Herr Volpert walked to a table set under one of the shop's two windows, where a tanned, russet cowhide was spread. He picked up a leather knife, a piece of chalk, and a pattern for a shoe's sole, and handed them to Christian.

"Christian," he said. "I'll start you on some cutting for now. You can use this whole hide for soles."

Christian looked at him in surprise.

"That will make a lot of shoes, sir," he said.

"Not nearly enough," answered the older man, with a bright, hard look at Christian. "These are for the Continental Army."

Christian felt a tightening twist at his midsection as Herr Volpert returned to his customer. It made sense, of course. A prisoner would naturally be put to work for the enemy cause. He stared at the tanned hide, and weighed the leather knife in his hand. Shoes for the enemy — how could he do it?

In that moment's speculation, he raised his eyes to the window, just in time to see Margaret run through the rain in the yard outside, with a bucket in each hand, and disappear into the cowshed opposite. And suddenly, an image of her flashed through his mind — not as she was now among her family, safely tidy and prim, but as she had been a month earlier, dirty and upset — facing down a wounded

88

patriot soldier in defense of the "enemy," Christian. He breathed deeply, once. Then he laid aside the knife, placed the stiff pattern on the leather, and began the process of tracing dozens of boot soles.

II

In the days and weeks that followed, Christian suited himself to the Volperts' routine; but he seemed hardly to touch their lives, or even to exist for them, except in his relentless cobbling work. Not that it was a bad life. They fed him well and never physically abused him. But sometimes in the solitary darkness of his loft, he found himself wishing for a solid place where he could stake a claim and stand. His longing blew him like the leaf-strewn winds of that November and early December of 1777, but where it would finally take him was still to be seen.

Gradually, though, Herr Volpert began to relieve the tedium of work with quiet conversation. Before long, the two men were comparing histories. They discovered that their forebears could easily have fought in the same Jäger regiments through the European wars of the previous generation. They knew many places in common, and even a few names.

Charlotte, too, breezed in and out of the shop with shoe pegs or messages, pastries or summonses, and it seemed that she brought a promise of summer and better days with her cheerful smile, happy chatter, and occasional mischief. Always she sidled up to Christian's bench, sometimes wondering what he was doing, sometimes wanting to know more about his home or his life before Reading. Christian shied away from long conversation, the memory of the marble episode always near the surface. But after a while, he began to look for trinkets and oddments of one kind or another that he could offer the child when she came calling.

Once, he brought a long, shimmering green feather he'd found one market day in Reading. When Charlotte appeared at his side offering a warm raisin tart in her chubby hand, he drew the feather out from where he'd hidden it in his sleeve with the air of a magician. Charlotte rewarded him with a sparkling "Oh! Oh!" and a quicksilver kiss on his cheek. Long after she had returned to the house, Christian worked with extra verve and a smile.

Then, on one of those rare December days that harken back to a warmer, sunnier season, a new distraction shook the safe monotony of Christian's life. The womenfolk filled the conversation at breakfast with their plans for the annual goosepicking: Wasn't the weather just as it should be, windless and warm? And who would be the fastest picker this year? The Scheffers and the Mumbergs were coming, and Christian gathered that the event was viewed by all as a minor holiday. Hard work it might be, but at least the week's normal rhythm was forced to skip a beat.

The men had hardly begun their cobbling when the sound of male voices from the yard brought Herr Volpert to sharp attention. The shop door swung open, then, and Carl Scheffer strode in with George close behind. Christian was struck, as he had been from his first sight of George, with a slippery sense of recognition.

"Any news?" Herr Volpert asked before the other man could speak.

"Maybe," interjected George. "Or another false rumor — like the British on the road to Reading."

"We'll see no Redcoats in Reading this winter," said Herr Scheffer. "They're too well set up with the Philadelphia Loyalists to care about a winter campaign this year. They live better than we do, with the traitors bowing and scraping to make them comfortable."

"Scandalous," murmured George, so quietly that only Christian could hear.

"What else have you heard, Carl?" asked Herr Volpert with unconcealed impatience.

"Well, I believe it may be good news for you," the man answered as he drew a stool up to the wood stove. "The colonel tells us the wounded in the New Jersey hospitals — the ones, you know, from the battle at Germantown — two thousand Americans dead or wounded, Frederick, can you imagine? Sometimes I wonder —"

"Carl," said Herr Volpert with a sigh, "this is not news — it happened in October — and it's not good."

"Oh," said Herr Scheffer, with the look of a man waking up. "Yes, of course. My point is that the wounded who are presently in New Jersey are being evacuated to other hospitals, including the Moravian hospital in Bethlehem."

"They can't!" blurted Christian without thinking. "There's no room for more. There isn't room for the men already there."

Herr Scheffer looked at Christian as though he had just

heard a chair speak to him. Christian quickly lowered his head over his work.

"He's right, Carl," said Herr Volpert. "I wish you'd get to this *good* news of yours. What you've told me so far is worth only tears."

"I'm sorry, Frederick," said his friend. "I get worked up. Colonel Boehm came to us today to tell us to ready our courthouse as a hospital. Some of Bethlehem's patients are being moved here to make space there. I've been asked to act as one of the escorts."

"And?" urged Herr Volpert.

"And," continued Herr Scheffer, with a sudden grin, "I'll see that John comes with me! You will have him home for Christmas!"

Christian's leather knife dropped from his hand to the floor with a clatter. As the three other men turned to look, he quickly bent to retrieve it. By the time he straightened, they had forgotten him again. No one noticed his shaking hands as he resumed his work.

Herr Volpert laid aside a half-made boot and rose swiftly, sidestepping his bench to reach his friend by the stove.

"Carl, I apologize," he said with a smile Christian had never seen before. "You couldn't have brought me better news if you'd told me the war was over!" With that, he threw his arms around the other man and gave him several mighty slaps on the back. "Come, we'll celebrate ahead of time. I have some fine rum I've been saving for something important."

The two men went out, laughing and congratulating one another.

But George lingered. When they were alone, he spoke to Christian in a low, conspiratorial voice. "Sometime you and I should talk. It can't be easy for you here."

This sounded more like a question than a statement, but Christian remained silent. George regarded him without expression.

"Well, I'll go now," he said. "Maybe I'll stop by sometime when you're not so busy, hm-m?"

With that, he left. Christian watched out the window until he saw George crossing the yard. There, each of the women had a goose on the ground in front of her, its head firmly caught inside a goose basket to keep it from biting or running away. The women plucked feathers systematically, stuffing them in large sacks to be used later for beds and quilts. The air was white with fluffy, floating goose down, as were the pickers themselves. As Christian watched, Margaret's goose began a wild flapping and honking that made the group in the yard laugh uproariously while the air became even thicker with plumage. Alone at his bench, Christian felt a familiar heaviness in his chest. He sighed and lowered his eyes to his work once more.

III

December passed rapidly and the Volperts waited. They asked the same questions of each other endlessly: Would John be transferred with the other wounded men from Bethlehem? Would he be able to endure the difficult trip with Carl?

When not talking about John, their conversation turned

to Jacob, quartered in the makeshift camp at Valley Forge — only thirty miles from Reading. Reports were bad and a single letter from Jacob did nothing to dispel them. He did include a hopeful postscript, however. He had volunteered, he explained, to travel to Reading with Henry Muller, another native of the town, on a foraging expedition for boots and food. They would have little time, so they planned to make it as close as possible to Christmas. With any luck, he'd be home on the holiday.

The day of Christmas Eve arrived without a sign of Jacob. Frau Volpert and Margaret prepared the house and the table for the holiday. They worked slowly and quietly, their mood at variance with the scene they created. They had lost hope of Jacob and had gone ahead to gather the household and set the first candles ablaze against encroaching dusk, when jarring thuds against the barred front door brought all of them to their feet. Herr Volpert opened the door cautiously, then threw it wide with an exclamation. Through the doorway stumbled Jacob, wet clumps of snow streaming down his blue cheeks and forming ice puddles on his hunched shoulders. More shocking than his appearance was the weight that bowed his shoulders; for close in his arms, he clutched John, who hung limp as a woman in a faint.

"Jacob, what is this?" cried his father.

"Quick Papa, he's frozen solid, I think," Jacob exclaimed. He stumbled into the room and across to his parents' bed.

The group burst into a flurry of horrified concern. Frau Volpert whirled to John's side, dragging off his drenched clothing and substituting one of her husband's heavy linen nightshirts.

"How did this happen?" she demanded of Jacob. "Where did you come from?"

Jacob pulled a chair close to John's bed and sat shivering, with his chapped hand on his brother's arm. His own drenched uniform steamed in the warm room, giving off a pungent smell.

"Henry and I just got to town. He'd left me for home, when I saw the hospital caravan down Market Street. I went to see what it was and Herr Scheffer noticed me."

"How could they bring them in such weather!" cried Frau Volpert. Herr Volpert carried in extra blankets from upstairs and lifted John while Frau Volpert and Jacob wrapped him well.

"They were trying for Christmas, like all of us," Jacob said.

All the while, Margaret tried to coax Jacob away from his brother's side, then finally brought hot rum and thick slabs of bread to him where he sat. Most of the rum went to John, but Jacob wolfed the bread as though he hadn't eaten in days.

Herr Volpert stoked the stove fire to white heat, while Charlotte hopped from one person to the next, making a pretty nuisance of herself between constant questions and wholehearted hugs for Jacob and John.

Only Christian stood apart, a reluctant witness to the family's distress. Herr Volpert had sent him for a load of wood. He returned unnoticed and carefully stacked the fuel. His throat ached and his hands sweated. He stared at the Christmas tree in the corner of the room, bedecked but unlit.

He didn't realize John had spoken until Margaret tapped his arm.

"Christian," she said, almost whispering. "John is talking to you."

Christian stared stupidly at her. Margaret's eyes glittered with reflected candlelight and the hint of tears.

"Won't you answer him?" she asked.

Christian fought an urge to run from the room, his eyes still locked with Margaret's. Only with great effort did he finally turn his gaze to the young man in the parlor bed.

John was coughing deep, choking barks. He lay curled on his side with one arm pressed hard across his stomach. When the spasm passed and he opened his eyes, he seemed to search the room. His gaze stopped at Christian.

"Who are you?" he asked, evidently repeating the question Christian had missed the first time. John sounded nearly done in, but he smiled.

It was the smile that closed Christian's throat. When he opened his mouth to answer, nothing came out. All he could think was, *I did it to you.* Christian looked from one Volpert to another in alarm. Everyone watched him, waiting.

Suddenly, Charlotte ran over from the group by the bed and grabbed Christian's hand in both of hers.

"Tell him, Christian," she insisted with a small, worried frown. She shook his hand and nodded emphatically. Christian raised his eyes once more from his young friend's face to that of her oldest brother's, that dream-familiar face with the blue, blue eyes, and finally, his vocal chords relaxed. He took a quick breath, stood at attention and spoke.

"Private Christian Theodor Sigismund Molitor, sir. Hessian prisoner of war." John's eyebrows quirked, but his weary smile never faltered. Christian swallowed and added,

"Presently serving as shoemaker for the Continental Army, sir."

A light seemed to dawn across John's face.

"A-a-ah," he said, still smiling. "Now I remember. You're Margaret's Hessian."

IV

The Volperts' Christmas Eve was given over to the elemental struggle for John's survival. Presents were forgotten, traditions unthought of. Yet Christmas Day brought hope like the pale winter morning, and in its first groping light, the family assembled around a rallying John. Frederick decided that his tribe would forgo the ritual, snowy trek to the Lutheran church.

"We'll have our own service of remembrance and thanksgiving here," he said, "where John can be included."

It was John himself who amended the plan to include Christian.

"We can't leave him alone for Christmas," John said. "This is a day of gifts. It we can't give, we don't deserve to receive."

His mother's mouth dropped open, but before she could speak, Charlotte had dashed out the back door. She returned alone. The Hessian had declined with all due respect.

"There! You see?" said Mama, and she marched out to the kitchen.

"What do you mean, he'd rather stay in his room?" demanded Jacob from his back-tilted chair by the wood stove. He took an enormous bite out of his Christmas pastry and continued to speak around the mouthful. "What kind of idiot would want to spend Christmas by himself?"

"Maybe he just doesn't want to spend it with us," said Charlotte from the floor, where she lay arranging a small pile of shoe pegs in front of her.

She positioned one too many pegs on her heap and it collapsed.

"*You* should go ask him, Margaret," said John, with a smile. She turned a startled gaze on her oldest brother.

"I . . . I couldn't," she stammered.

"Why not?" John asked. Margaret stared at him a moment in near panic. Then her expression cleared.

"Mama needs my help," she asserted, then bolted for the kitchen in a swish of dress linen.

She listened from the hearth to the parlor discussion that followed. Papa suggested that Christian be left alone if that was what he wanted. But the soldiers disagreed. They had suffered the separation from everything familiar and loved. John, in particular, had spent last Christmas doing battle. Surely, Christmas with any family was better than solitude. Finally, the young men won the day — Papa retraced Charlotte's steps and was soon ushering Christian in at the door.

John was too weak to come to the table, so they moved the table and all its finery to him. His mother fussed at him because he hardly ate his breakfast, and Jacob sat as close to his side as he could. After his first choking attempt, John didn't join the others in singing favorites from their German hymnbook. At one point, Margaret noticed Christian staring at him, and barely singing. Unexpectedly, John met his gaze, and Christian seemed suddenly to lose the thread of the familiar carol's refrain. A look of unease flashed across his face before he lowered his eyes in confusion.

Before the last carol had quite faded, Charlotte draped herself around her father's neck, pleading for the gift opening they had postponed the night before.

"All right, *Liebchen*," he said. "We'll get the presents."

Papa and Mama disappeared into the kitchen, returning moments later with their arms full of the season's tokens, something for each of their children. Alongside sweetmeats and gingerbread, Charlotte and Margaret each opened small baskets full of bright homemade pleasures.

Charlotte popped a small cake into her mouth, while Margaret enthused over the set of bone hairbrushes, hand-painted with tiny rose and lavender flowers, that had been her grandmother's. Jacob and John were each presented with a sturdy new pair of boots. Jacob bent immediately to try his on, but John merely lay back with his pair in his lap.

"I'll use them for the spring planting," he said, then fell to coughing. When he'd recovered, silence enveloped the group — and into that quiet, Charlotte suddenly chirped, "Where's Christian's gifts?"

A new silence followed, a long, uncomfortable stillness. No one had thought to give Christian a Christmas present. In fact, since the gifts had been brought out, no one had thought about Christian at all. Now, after Charlotte's question, he was at the center of their thoughts. And there he sat in his corner, looking most awkward of all.

Charlotte looked around the circle of her family, and realized the truth. She looked at her own small heap of presents. Carefully, she lifted the basket full of sweets and stood. Her mother would have stopped her except for Papa's interference. Charlotte crossed the room unhindered to her friend. With both hands, she held her basket out to Christian.

"Happy Christmas," she said solemnly. Christian slowly reached to take the little girl's gift.

"Happy Christmas," he answered, equally grave.

Mama raised a hand to her suddenly moist eyes. Margaret felt her own eyes fill and looked away, biting her lip, while her brothers sat with steady gazes leveled at the floor. Frederick cleared his throat and moved to load the wood stove though it was already full and burning hot.

The moment would have been unbearable, if it had lasted any longer; but it was broken by the sharp knock on the door. Margaret breathed a thankful sigh as she jumped to her feet and rushed to push back the long iron bolt. As she swung open the door, a river of cold spilled into the room leaving Henry Muller in its wake, his face ruddied and damp with fine snow. He'd come for Jacob.

Jacob rose to gather his belongings even while Henry and the Volperts greeted one another.

"Surely you can stay for hot grog!" insisted Anna Maria.

"If we hadn't promised to hurry back to Valley Forge with boots and food," Jacob explained, "we wouldn't have gotten leave to come to Reading at all."

"One drink," his mother pressed.

"Perhaps one," said Henry, and Anna Maria hurried off to bring a second breakfast. For a short hour longer, Christmas would prevail.

Leave-taking that noontime was harder than ever.

"I wish I could have made this morning last a year," Jacob

murmured to Margaret as the time approached. He held up his cup of rum in one hand, a piece of sweet bread in the other. "But every time I feel the warmth of this sliding down, it reminds me of how cold I was, this time yesterday!"

"And you think of the others waiting for you," Margaret added. "I know. It's when I'm most comfortable that I think of the Moravian hospital."

Jacob gave his sister a steady, almost surprised, look. Then he reached out and pulled on a loose strand of her hair.

"You're coming along, Margaret," he said. "You really are!"

Jacob and Henry departed on horseback, with the Volperts' sled hitched behind Jacob's horse, loaded with crates of boots. After they passed out of sight, the day's cheer seemed to leave as well, and the celebration came to an end.

Dinner came and went quietly. Christian slipped off as soon as he politely could, while the Volperts worked to make John more comfortable for the long rest he would certainly need. Only toward evening did Margaret finally have time to think. As she pushed a needle in and out, in and out, of a much-mended shirt, Jacob's comment suddenly popped into her mind.

"You're coming along," he had said. Now what did he mean by that?

Chapter Six

I *shouldn't be here,* Christian thought many times in the weeks that followed John's coming home. *If they knew I'd done this to him, they wouldn't have me.*

The daily spectacle of John's suffering shadowed Christian's waking hours, and his own vivid dreams accused him in his sleep. He choked on the Volperts' food, wore John's and Jacob's clothes like hair shirts, even lost the small joy he'd known in Charlotte's favor — she gazed at him with blue Volpert eyes, one more reproach.

Then one day, John asked to be moved upstairs to his own bed. He said the family's constant coming and going exhausted him. So Herr Volpert asked Christian to help carry John up the stairs, and afterward John asked if he wouldn't stay for a short time and share something hot to drink.

John was too tired to talk with Christian for long that first visit, but the next day a bewildered-looking Margaret appeared midafternoon at the shop door.

"Christian," she said in an odd, tentative voice. She rarely addressed him, and his name sounded awkward on her lips. "John has asked if you would please join him in his room for dinner."

Christian sat in silent confusion, not knowing how to respond.

"Go, by all means," Herr Volpert said, though he too seemed puzzled.

So Christian made his way back to the attic sickroom. Once again, the visit was short, but the acute embarrassment Christian had suffered the first time began to wane. The following day, John asked him again.

Before long, John made such a daily pattern of the invitation, that he no longer had to ask. Frau Volpert simply handed Christian a tray set for two as he passed through the kitchen on his way up the narrow stairs to her ailing son's bedside. She voiced no objections, but never once did she look Christian in the eye or speak to him directly. If she needed to communicate something, Margaret acted as messenger.

Meanwhile, Christian found himself talking more freely to John, not only of his past, but of the present. John was full of questions about Germany and the Hessian army. And Christian had a consuming curiosity about the Americans.

"You mustn't call us rebels," John said with a smile one day. "At least not while you're with us. Not out loud. It's a relief to have another army man to talk to, but I can't be hearing that all the time."

"I beg your pardon," answered Christian stiffly. "I was trained to believe it."

"Don't be offended," said John. "I'm trying to help."

After that, Christian found it easier to talk on any subject. Only when John spoke of the battle at Brandywine did he turn once more ill at ease.

"Did you fight there, too?" John asked him.

Christian felt a tightening in his chest as he stared into John's drawn face. The mention of Brandywine inevitably brought his sleeping sense of guilt to the surface. He answered John with a quiet "*ja.*"

"Strange to think of the two of us fighting on opposing sides in that, isn't it?" continued John. "That's where I got it, you know."

"Oh, *ja.* I mean, I guess I knew that . . . someone said . . . ," Christian faded off.

"When were you wounded?" John persisted gently.

"I . . . it was there, too," faltered Christian.

John backed away from the topic then and didn't bring it up again. Yet for one heart-thumping moment, Christian had been deeply tempted to blurt out the truth. By then, though, John had changed the subject, and Christian lost his opportunity and his nerve.

Despite his nagging self-accusation, however, the afternoon interviews became the highlight of Christian's days. He liked it best when John did the talking. John seemed to know so much and to be so sure.

"How can you complain about taxes?" asked Christian, one day, voicing one of the many questions that had bothered him since he first understood that these "rebels" were neither as lawless nor as murderous as he had been told. "Your king sent an army to protect you from the Indians and from the French. Shouldn't you help pay for that?"

"But we had no say! We have a right to be represented in Parliament if we're going to pay taxes," John explained. "If we're only a colony of slaves, then we'll do without a tyrant king and his army and govern ourselves. We've done it already. We can go on doing it."

"But that means chaos!" cried Christian.

John smiled. He gestured out his small dormer window.

"You've been out and about, Christian," he said more quietly. "Is that what you see? Chaos?"

Christian had no answer to that; he did not see anarchy in Reading, or anywhere else in his experience of America, only a people who appointed officials, made and kept their laws, prosecuted offenders, and, in every practical way, lived in order and internal peace.

The discussions continued, and Christian daily descended the steep stairs with a lighter step than he had climbed them.

In this happy frame of mind, Christian one day bade a cheerful farewell to John and strode out of the room so quickly that he nearly collided with Margaret, who was standing just outside. He caught himself at the last possible moment by grabbing the doorjamb and the wall for balance.

"I beg your pardon!" he said and swallowed against a sudden thick feeling in his throat.

Margaret had jumped back a half pace.

"That's all right," she said, sounding breathless. "I was just in my room and . . . uh . . . I . . ."

She stopped speaking and gave a peculiar little shrug. After an uncomfortable moment, she added, "I'm going to look in on John." Then she hurried past Christian with a brush of a glance and the faintest whiff of a scent that might have been ginger or some woody flower.

Christian returned to the workshop more slowly than usual. Was his imagination overworking, or had Margaret actually been standing for some time right where he found her, listening in the hall? Now why, he asked himself as he settled at his workbench, would she do that?

II

After that day, Margaret regularly offered a word of greeting to Christian when they met, which irresistibly elicited his smile. As though some evil spell had been broken by John's arrival, Christian's loneliness dropped from his shoulders. Gestures of friendship seemed to come from every side, and Christian basked in their warmth.

The next time George Scheffer stopped in the shop, it seemed natural that he'd extend some friendly interest.

"Where is everybody?" asked George after a polite exchange of greetings.

"They all went on a shopping expedition," answered Christian with a smile. "Except John, of course."

He pulled tight on the boot stitching in front of him, while George drew up a nearby stool. When George continued the small talk, Christian relaxed into the conversation with an ease born of his daily dialogue with John.

The talk turned to the war, as it always did these days.

"I suppose you've heard the latest news," George said.

"Which news is that?" asked Christian. He pulled another stitch through the tough leather.

"Why, the treaty," said George.

"What treaty?" asked Christian, poking the needle into the next hole.

Silence followed, until Christian finally looked up to see why George didn't answer. The American sat with arms folded, legs crossed, and his head cocked to one side.

"They keep you rather in the dark, don't they?" he said sympathetically. "Or perhaps they wanted to spare you the bad news."

"What treaty?" repeated Christian.

"The treaty with France," said George. "The 'Treaty of Amity and Alliance.' The British aren't just fighting the Americans, now. They're also at war with the second most powerful nation in the world: France!"

"France!" echoed Christian. "But America could *win* if France helps!"

"True," George agreed.

"What's the American side of the bargain?" asked Christian, his shoemaking suddenly forgotten.

"Ah," said George with one finger wagging at Christian. "That's the question, isn't it? The Americans need only — *only*, mind you — promise never to make peace with England by becoming her subjects again."

Christian's mind was full of images — of his own experiences under the British officers, so sure of their superiority and victory; of the American soldiers sniping desperately from hedgerows at the orderly ranks of Hessian soldiers; of the bloody British victory at Brandywine; of Jacob Volpert and Henry Muller driving away with their inadequate load of boots to the winter nightmare of Valley Forge; and of John, lying in bed day after day, most alive when he was explaining to Christian a royal subject's right to resist tyranny and seek independence.

"It's the worst blow to England's cause since Baron von Steuben took over the training and drilling of the Continental Army," said George. With every point he made, he became more intense, and Christian's confusion grew.

"For your people to hold their ground," continued George slowly, "they'll need all their skill and some well-placed friends."

As he spoke these last words, George stared keenly at Christian.

"You could be one of those friends, Christian," he continued after a short silence.

"Me?" asked Christian, warily. "What are you talking about?"

George leaned forward, clenching his hands on his knees, his expression as tight as his fists and his voice low.

"You're in a position to hear things," he said, almost whispering. "Jacob comes and goes and he's close to important people, people in the know. Herr Volpert, too." George leaned even closer to Christian. "You may *already* have information that could be of use to the British effort.

And listen to me now — I know where to take it so that it can be made to count!"

Christian gaped in silence at this lifelong friend of the Volpert family, but before he could even collect his thoughts, there was a noise in the yard and the shop door was flung open.

"Christian!" cried Margaret with a laugh. "You must come directly! Frau Stern is stuck in the mud out front, and Papa can't budge her! Oh!" she added at the sight of George.

"Margaret, *guten Tag*," said George, rising and crossing the room to her side. "Perhaps I can help."

Margaret stiffened visibly as George tried to take her arm. His first warm response turned to a hard smile as he let his hand drop to his side.

"Papa asked for Christian," Margaret explained in a small voice.

"We'll all go," said George. He turned a closed face to Christian. "Shall we?"

Christian rose and followed reluctantly, pulling on his jacket as he went. George nodded to Margaret to go ahead. She hesitated, glanced at Christian, then preceded the men in silence. Just as they reached the front gate and the spectacle of the Stern carriage leaning dangerously in the mud, George turned and spoke so that only Christian could hear.

"We'll talk again, soon," he said. As he turned and walked away, an old memory stirred in Christian, one from before Brandywine. He saw again the brief glimpse of a solitary horseman, an American civilian, riding through the Jäger encampment, and he knew why George had seemed familiar from the start — George and that mysterious rider were one and the same.

III

Through the winter and spring of 1778, Christian clung to the growing acceptance he felt among the Volperts as to a lifeline, and they in turn clung to routine. Margaret, like the rest, picked up the threads of habit, milking and mending, baking and quilting her way through the cold months; and digging into the thawed earth as soon as it would receive her attention. Woven into the pattern like a dark-hued strand was John's care, shared primarily by Margaret and her mother, and more work than ever as his condition worsened. The closer, warmer air of late spring made the climb upstairs more troublesome to Mama, so that Margaret carried the bulk of the nursing.

One afternoon in June, Margaret climbed to John's room with the water pitcher for his washstand. The summer air was so heavy, she felt she carried its weight more ponderously than she did the jug's. As she reached the top of the stairs, she could hear Christian's voice. She stopped short of the doorway as she often did, listening and resting against the cool wall.

"Another group of English prisoners left the prison camp this morning," she heard Christian saying. "The tanner said they've been exchanged for American prisoners in New York."

"Any of your Hessians go?" asked John. His voice cracked and he coughed.

"No, not one," said Christian. His voice rose. "John, I've

talked to some of them. They say the British only set up exchanges for English soldiers. They say King Frederick doesn't want us back."

"Do you believe that?" asked John. "Why wouldn't he want his own soldiers back?"

"They're saying he can't support us if we aren't fighting," answered Christian. "Some of the Jägers have never done anything but soldier. They wouldn't know how to do anything else."

"Surely they could learn."

"Not if they aren't given a chance," said Christian.

"Well, anyway," said John. "That doesn't apply to you. You have a trade. When the war is over, you can sail home and be sure of a welcome — if that's what you want."

"I'm not sure I can," said Christian slowly. "It's as though we aren't really King Frederick's people, just goods for trade to keep his coffers full."

"Like King George and those of us in the colonies."

John said this last with the suggestion of a question. Margaret waited silently for Christian's response. But the next voice she heard startled her from behind instead.

"What are you doing out here in the hall?" piped Charlotte. Margaret jumped and lost her grip on the china jug. It smashed on the wooden tread and every splintering shard raised its separate hue and cry.

"Oh Lottie!" Margaret cried. "Look what you've done, sneaking up like that!"

"Me!" cried Charlotte. She raised her chin, viewing the wreckage down her snub nose. Then she stepped gingerly around Margaret to John's door.

"One of these days," Margaret muttered, as she cleared the second step with her foot and dropped to her knees there. She'd begun to fill her apron with the larger pieces of the shattered pitcher when her elbow was taken in a firm grip.

"Don't you do that," said Christian. He pulled her to her feet. "Look. You've gotten your dress all wet. Let me get the broom."

Margaret's apron slipped out of her hand as she rose and, for a second time, pottery crashed. She stared at her dripping skirt.

"Please don't," she said. "It's my mess."

"Margaret yelled at me, Johnny," said Charlotte clearly from John's room, with a quaver in her voice.

"I'll be back with the broom in a minute," said Christian. He crunched past Margaret and down the littered stairs. As soon as he'd gone, John called out.

"Margaret! Please come here."

Margaret stepped carefully over the debris and into John's room, her palms pressed against her burning cheeks. John spoke to Charlotte, sitting on the bed beside him.

"Be a good girl and fetch me some of Mama's honey tea. My throat's on fire," he said.

"But I want to stay here!" she cried, closer than ever to tears.

"Please, Lottie," said her brother, and in truth, he sounded as though he needed some relief. Charlotte gazed at his wasted face, her inward battle reflected on her young features. Then she gave a quick, shaky sigh.

"All right," she said gently. She leaned forward and gave

John a careful kiss on his cheek, so careful that Margaret was inclined to forgive her the smashed pitcher.

When Charlotte had gone, Margaret took her place on John's bed. He rested back against his pillow with his eyes closed. "Margaret?"

"Yes, Johnny?" she answered. She reached forward and pushed his hair away from his eyes.

"Why are you so hard on Christian?" John asked. He opened his eyes and watched Margaret intently, almost feverishly, taking her hand in his.

"Hard on him?" she said in confusion. "What do you mean?"

"I see you. Whenever he's around you. One minute you're smiling and sweet to him, the next you're ice-cold. That's tough on a man. Especially when he has an interest."

"I'm not!" she said. Then, "He doesn't!" She clapped a hand over her mouth at the sound of footsteps on the stairs, followed by the sweep of the broom. She leaned closer to John, suddenly breathless, and whispered, "How do you know?"

"I'm a man. I know," he whispered back with a wink she hadn't seen for a long time. "And you like him."

"Of course I like him," she said, still in an undertone. She tried to meet him stare for stare, but finally turned away.

"I mean *really* like him, Margaret," said John. He shook her hand so she would look at him again. "So why don't you let him know it?"

Margaret frowned at her brother and picked at the hem of her apron with restless fingers.

113

"He's a Hessian," she said at last.

"So was our grandfather," retorted John with unusual energy.

"Mama would be furious," she said, and realized as soon as she said it that this wasn't a new thought to her.

"Mama would get over it," answered John. When he spoke again, he seemed to deliberate over every word. "Sometimes, Margaret, you have to decide for yourself what is right, and act on it, no matter what other people say."

Margaret mentally picked this up, turning it one way, then another, with the sense that she handled a sort of key, if only she could get a proper hold on it. There was a knock at the door.

"Yes!" called John. That simple act seemed to break his momentary spell of vitality. He wheezed into a long coughing breath that hacked through his entire frame.

"Excuse me," said Christian, speaking through the barely opened door. "I thought you'd want to know. Jacob just arrived downstairs."

John asked to be taken to the kitchen. Jacob and Christian enthroned him in the best chair, and his mother wrapped him well despite the heat of the late afternoon. The sun streamed through the windows in long, parallel shafts, and caught the ingathering of the Volperts in its rhythm of light and shadow.

Once again, Jacob came in desperate search of boots, though the soldiers were on the other side of a miserable winter at Valley Forge, with some strong military advances to boost morale.

"We didn't win at Monmouth," Jacob was saying. "But we didn't lose either. We fought well together, thanks to von Steuben and his eternal drills. The British couldn't budge us."

He turned to John.

"We marched for seven days. Every morning, the fog was impossible, the way it was at Brandywine." John nodded. "Every afternoon, my tongue felt too swollen for me to swallow, it was so hot. But even with all that, we shadowed Clinton's troops the whole way north from Philadelphia.

"The heat never let up. We were ready to drop. But we pressed on, anyway, and I swear we were in near-perfect order! We took the high ground by the courthouse and we held it."

He went on to tell a story that had circulated of the wife of one of his privates — tiny Mary Hays. All through that torrid day's fighting, she had carried jugs of water to the thirsty men, so that those watching began calling her "Molly Pitcher." In the worst of the afternoon, the legend had it, Mary's husband was overcome by the heat. Mary laid aside her water jug, stepped over her prostrate husband, and took his place by the cannon, loading and firing until nightfall.

As Margaret listened, she saw the scene in her imagination, and imagined, too, how she would have helped if she'd been there. Then her glance fell on Christian, who was following Jacob's every word intently.

"We'll win," Jacob asserted. "There's no question now. We'll win!"

Christian stirred in his seat as though uncomfortable, and

Margaret thought he was about to speak. But then John started to cough, and Christian shut his mouth to a thin line and bowed his head.

IV

Jacob's visit was a great relief to his family. With relief grew hope that lasted throughout that summer and into the fall, as no new reports of battles arrived.

John's condition, though, was another story, and he had greater need of Margaret's help in the sickroom. As a result, she saw even more of Christian than before. In fact, as the harvest days shortened, and everyone was more often at home, brother, sister, and Hessian frequently made a threesome in the small attic room.

One crisp November market day, however, Margaret planned an excursion to town, an unusual event in her present life.

"Mama, where's Papa?" she asked from the stairs. She fastened her cape tight at her neck as she walked into the kitchen. "He promised to drive me to the Hessian prison camp, but I can't find him anywhere."

"He must have forgotten," her mother replied. She fussed over a bubbling pot, with an array of dried flowers and herbs spread before her on the hearth. Breaking off a piece of one of the herbs, she sprinkled the tiniest amount into the pot. She muttered something under her breath, then added, "Anyway, he just left for supplies."

"Oh, Mama, no!" cried Margaret. "I can't wait until next market day to fetch the bandages and vinegar."

Margaret paused, waiting. Mama carefully stirred her concoction with one of her few silver spoons. "Mama, what are you doing?" Margaret finally asked. She could feel sweat forming on her upper lip and under her cape. "Mama!"

After a pause, her mother looked up in surprise. Margaret repeated her question.

"Barbara Mumberg has given me a new recipe for a cure," she said. "If I don't pay attention to what I'm doing, I'll get it wrong and it won't do John any good at all. I wish you'd talk to me later!" She selected another herb and pinched a bit of it into her brew.

"But what about the supplies from the Lutheran ladies?" demanded Margaret. "Mama, I *promised!*"

Mama made an impatient wave at her, a shooing motion that said plainly, "Go away."

Margaret turned abruptly and marched out of the house. Outside, the brittle air instantly reduced her overheated temperature, but her anger still left warmth in her cheeks. And as her eyes and nose began to burn from the dry, cold air, her impatience grew. She could see the tail end of the horse through the open cowshed door, and the wagon propped against the side of the workshop, so her father must have walked. Margaret's attention moved from the upended wagon to the shop chimney. The sun's first rays shot over the rooftop and lit up the straight pillar of smoke streaming skyward.

An idea glimmered in Margaret's mind. She hesitated, her gaze dropping to the workshop entrance, then glanced over her shoulder at the kitchen door. Her heart began to pound as she crossed the yard and knocked lightly at the shop door, quickly letting herself in. Christian straightened where he stood by the open wood stove.

"*Guten Morgen*," said Margaret with a tentative smile. Christian returned the greeting and the smile.

"Your father's not here," he added.

"I know," said Margaret. She continued in a sudden rush. "Christian, I need to go to town in the wagon. But I can't drive it. Would . . . would you please help me?"

Christian stared, perfectly still, then appeared to collect himself.

"Yes!" he said, a trifle loudly. He added more quietly, "Of course."

Only after he'd agreed did Margaret realize she'd been holding her breath while he decided. While they hitched up horse and wagon, and then rolled out of the dooryard, she glanced every few seconds at the kitchen windows and door. Never had it taken so long or made such a racket to ready that wagon! It was a small miracle that Mama hadn't appeared to investigate.

As the wagon moved along Prince Street, a silence fell between the two young travelers. In all their meetings in John's room, and even in the hospital in Bethlehem, they'd never been alone together. Margaret could think of nothing to say.

Without warning, Christian started to laugh. Margaret looked at him in surprise.

"Where are we going?" he asked.

"Oh my!" she said and started to giggle. "I forgot to tell you, didn't I?"

After she'd explained her mission of mercy, taking medical

supplies donated by the church women to the Hessian prison camp outside the town, the pair lapsed into another, more comfortable, silence that lasted until they reached the market. Once they had fetched and loaded the waiting supplies, they headed for the camp. Only then did Margaret disturb the wave of quiet they rode.

"Christian."

She hesitated, staring ahead at the horse's rhythmic, swinging pull. The mare's breath appeared in little puffs that quickly blew past her ears and disappeared. Now or never, Margaret thought suddenly.

"Christian," she repeated firmly, and turned in her seat to look at him. "There's something I need to say to you."

Christian threw her a wary glance, then looked back at the road.

"The time since you've been a prisoner must have been awful for you," Margaret continued. Her companion made a sort of half-nod, half-shrug.

"Not so awful now — and never for me the way it's been for the men in the prison camp," he said.

"But you must be lonely for your family. You've been with us for a year," she pressed. "And you have to work terribly hard."

"It's work I like doing, though," he said.

"Well, we haven't been very nice to you," Margaret insisted. "We've treated you like a servant — and sometimes worse."

"I haven't thought that," said Christian. "Your father is a kind employer, and John and the little one have always treated me as a friend."

"For heaven's sake, Christian!" exclaimed Margaret. He looked at her again, the first look since she'd opened the conversation. "I'm trying to apologize and all you do is argue with me!"

The two stared at each other, while the wagon bumped and swayed slowly along; then they were laughing — free, singing laughter that made their eyes water and their ribs ache. And when it had sung itself out, they looked at each other again quietly, then watched the slow passage of scenery with lingering smiles.

"Look!" cried Christian suddenly and he pointed upward.

Circling high in the crystal air above their heads was a beautiful bird — a broad-winged hawk — soaring wide and effortlessly on invisible currents.

"He's so lovely," sighed Margaret.

"He's so free," added Christian.

Their smiles persisted through their business at the Hessian camp, where Margaret dealt with the prisoners' wives while Christian waited and chatted with a few nearby Hessians. They continued for the ride home, during which the two wondered together over the prisoners in the camp, and the women and children who had followed their soldiers across the sea, through the battlegrounds, and into captivity. The Volperts' house appeared too soon.

Mama stood waiting in the dooryard, stone silent while they climbed out of the wagon. She ushered them wordlessly inside, and only when they stood eye to eye with her in her kitchen did she let loose the full storm of her feeling.

"Is this the way you thank the parents who love you?"

she demanded of Margaret. "Do you sneak and deceive as soon as you don't get your way?"

"But Mama, I didn't . . ."

"And *you*," she threw at Christian. "Do you think because you live here that you have become papa, or brother, to my daughter? Do you think —"

"Anna, what now!" said Papa from the door.

Her anger far from spent, Mama poured out her grief.

"Margaret?" asked Papa.

"I needed help and you were gone," she said quietly.

"Did you ask permission?"

"No, Papa."

"You owe your mama an apology. Next time, ask permission."

Such an end to their adventure became the beginning of a new one for Christian and Margaret. The smile that first colored Margaret's world that market day in November grew brighter over the cold winter months that followed into the new year of 1779. The most mundane of her chores seemed to take on the pleasure of an afternoon's stroll by the river, and she found herself gaily singing her way through her days. The times when she would see Christian — at meals, in John's room, or by the fire in the long evenings — became the center points around which everything else revolved. And their periodic excursions of mercy together to the Hessian camp, now sanctioned by Papa, fed in privacy what was taking unnoticed life in the company of others. As winter passed into spring, Margaret's spare thoughts turned almost always to Christian.

Chapter Seven

I

Was it her happy preoccupation over the course of half a year that blunted the foreboding in Margaret? Or had she simply refused to look at unkind reality? In either case, the day came that she strode into John's room and stared unexpectedly at appalling truth.

John lay on his side, curled around his tucked-in elbows with a handkerchief clutched in both hands. He breathed too noisily, and his lips and his fingernails were blue, his skin impossibly bloodless. In contrast, the blood on his handkerchief was all the more shocking. Margaret stopped in the doorway, and the thought emerged independent of its thinker.

He's dying, it whispered. *He's dying. He's dying.*

She tiptoed past him to the window, and clutched at the sill until her knuckles were the color of John's.

He's dying, whistled the summer wind past the hinges.
He's dying.

Outside, below, all was as it had been before, sunny but blustery. She searched for something that would make sense of John, lying so terribly sick. But she could find none, and its absence was a terrible insult to her love for him.

"Margaret."

She turned at the sound of John's wasted voice. His eyes were open now, but he seemed to stare through her, rather than at her.

"I'm thirsty," he said.

"Here Johnny," she said as she hurried to him. "I have broth for you."

She stayed longer than usual that day, reluctant as never before to leave him alone.

The next day, Jacob came home again on a two-day leave. Margaret could hardly take her eyes off him as he moved proudly in his fine, new uniform.

"I'll report on June twenty-eighth to a special new Light Infantry encampment," he announced over dinner. After a pause, he added, "As company commander under General Wayne."

He reached into his waistcoat and pulled out a packet that he handed to his father.

"That's the commission that goes with the promotion," he explained with a proud lift of his chin.

There followed dozens of questions. But Margaret listened with only one ear. She was wondering if Jacob realized how much John had worsened. And she was watching Christian, absorbed in Jacob's every comment. His avid attention reminded her of Jacob the year before he was allowed to enlist. Meanwhile, John slept fitfully upstairs, and she wanted to go up and check on him. What would be the end of all this?

Jacob, at least, knew what was next for him.

"The Light Infantry is an elite company," he was saying. "Hand-picked for size, intelligence, and discipline. We're all native-born to America, and most of us have drilled under Steuben. There's not a better unit in the American army."

"Like the Jäger corps," suggested Papa.

"Exactly," said Jacob, nodding. "Except that we'll be fighting for ourselves."

At that, Margaret saw Christian lower his eyes and stare at his hands where they rested on the table, his expression unreadable.

"And where are they sending you and your special friends?" asked Mama.

"Sandy Beach, Mama," answered Jacob. "It's on the Hudson River in New York, about five miles south of the fort at West Point."

"Will you fight?" she asked and her smile tightened. "Something must be happening for General Wayne to have such an exceptional group of soldiers."

Jacob hesitated, but his father joined in.

"Yes, son, what do you think they have in mind?"

"I can only guess," started Jacob slowly. "The British hold New York town and several forts up the Hudson. We've got West Point. But neither of us can move as things stand."

"So?" prompted Papa when Jacob paused again.

"Well, my *guess*," continued Jacob, "is that we'll try to capture at least one of those forts to weaken General Howe's stronghold on the river. The best bet would be Verplanck's Point or Stony Point."

"When?" demanded Charlotte, who'd been squirming in her seat throughout the conversation. Her eyes sparkled as she stared at her brother's new uniform.

"I have no idea!" said Jacob and started to laugh. "It's all guesswork. Who knows?"

Jacob's visit seemed to give wings to time and almost before Margaret knew it, she was waving him out of Reading again. He had spent as much time upstairs as John could stand, and he sat with his father and Christian in the workshop for hours the morning he left. Margaret wanted to be with him, too, but as always, the war seemed to draw the men close to one another while it shut her out of all but farewells.

That evening, George Scheffer came by with more boot orders. He refused Papa's invitation to a cup of ale with a polite thank you. Then he asked for Christian.

"The other day, he asked me about a tool they use in Germany," he explained. "I told him I'd look into it."

George was directed to the workshop. He bid the Volperts *guten Abend* and left. After a few minutes, Margaret stood and stretched, then wandered away from the family grouped around the single tallow lamp.

"I think I'll just step out and get a little air," she said.

Outside, Margaret walked silently in the shadow of the

house to the corner closest to the workshop. She could see no one through the lighted windows, but the open door allowed the voices to carry in the still evening.

"I'm sorry," Christian was saying. "I have nothing to offer you."

"But surely, Christian," said George, "with his visit to-day . . ."

"No!" said the Hessian, cutting George off. "Nothing at all."

"Perhaps if you just tell me . . ."

"I'm sorry."

There was a prolonged silence. Then the doorway darkened for a moment as George left with long, hard-heeled strides. Margaret pushed herself flat against the side of the house, hoping she blended with the dark. But George never glanced right or left. He opened the gate with a tug that threw it so vigorously against the fence that it bounced back and hit his heels before he was entirely out of its path. He swore as he turned and gave it a kick, and then he was gone. Margaret started toward the shop, but halfway across the yard, she hesitated, then stopped. It was none of her business. And maybe Christian would tell her without being asked.

II

June had brought full summer almost overnight. The day Christian drove Margaret yet again to the Hessian camp was brilliant and warm, the kind of day that seems to promise all the best of everything. The wagon ride seemed to fly, and Christian helped Margaret out at the guardhouse reluctantly.

After leaving her, he wandered through the camp, rambling his way to the tents by the river, where he could see some prisoners working in their gardens. One of the men hailed him and raised his hoe in salute.

"Molitor," the man called. "*Guten Tag.*"

Christian came abreast of Hans Guber, a fellow Jäger he'd gotten to know on earlier visits to the camp.

"*Guten Tag*, Hans," he replied. Christian glanced at the unfamiliar pair who worked alongside Hans and nodded.

The men, Hans explained as he made introductions, were new arrivals. Christian he described as a working prisoner of war. He added jokingly, "The Americans have nearly converted him to the other side, though. He's been making rebel noises of 'liberty from tyranny' around here that give some of the men ideas."

Before Christian could reply, one of the new prisoners tapped him lightly on the arm with the handle of his rake.

"I wouldn't rush into anything, Molitor," he said with a cocky lift of his eyebrows. "Things may not turn out the way you seem to think."

"What do you mean?" demanded Hans. "Did you hear something before you were caught — where was it? On the Hudson?"

"You guess well. I've heard the Americans would not do so well at West Point," he said. "We've got the lion's share of deployment from New York town and upriver toward West Point. Capturing it could leave them close to defeated."

The mention of West Point brought Jacob immediately to Christian's mind, riding confidently out of Reading in his Light Infantry uniform, heading for Sandy Beach. Christian remembered Jacob's speculations about Wayne's new troops and their secret mission.

"What makes you think the Americans will wait around to be attacked?" he asked.

"What choice do they have?" asked the prisoner. "They can't touch our forts!"

"I don't believe it," said Hans. "Even the river forts, themselves?"

"Especially those!" said the man who had done all the talking so far. "The defenses are first class."

"For the most part," murmured the other prisoner.

" 'For the most part'!" pressed Hans with a curious gleam in his eye. "You mean they're not complete? Well then, maybe Molitor has a point after all!"

"They are complete," asserted the first prisoner.

"Except Stony Point," added the other.

"There's only that one spot on the west end —" the first began.

At that point, Christian heard Margaret calling his name from the wagon. He tried to continue the conversation, but the others were staring off at Margaret, so he made his unwilling farewell. As he walked away, one of the men called after him, "Well, anyway, if you're looking for a winner, I wouldn't bet on the rebels, if I were you."

Christian helped Margaret into the wagon and urged the horse into a trot.

"You were faster than usual," Christian said absently, his mind still on what he had just heard.

"They wouldn't let me stay," Margaret answered gravely. "They have the fever!"

"Fever!" he repeated, fully attentive now. "Has anyone died?"

"Three," she answered, staring at him with wide eyes. "So far."

Hours later in the dark of his room, Christian's mind came back to his conversation with the prisoners. Suppose the Americans found out about Stony Point's weak spot? What if they moved to take advantage of it? If the prisoner was right, such an American victory could be the saving of West Point.

Wayne's elite corps was a secret, according to Jacob, and they might be planning an attack. Did the British know about them? Forewarned, the King's men could certainly cover the Stony Point weakness. They might even storm the American troops before they could mass for the attack.

If Jacob hadn't come home when he did with the news of his assignment, Christian thought, that piece of intelligence from the Hessians would have meant nothing to him. Yet here he lay, a prisoner of war — with information that could help or hinder either his own Hessian army or the country whose people and ideas he was growing to love.

But what to do with it? If only he could talk it out with someone! Margaret? He thought not. She seemed to lower a shade over her bright eyes, to retreat, whenever the subject of the war was raised.

Herr Volpert was a possibility. But Christian couldn't imagine talking to him about so deeply personal a dilemma. As kind as he'd been from the start, he was still Christian's master and an ardent patriot.

That left John. Even in his terrible weakness, he preached freedom to Christian at every opportunity. Surely he would want to hear about this. And just as surely, he would offer advice. With the decision made at last, Christian drifted into a restless sleep.

The next afternoon, he found John alert, as he'd hoped. He waited until Margaret was busy elsewhere, then seized the chance to tell John about the conversation at the Hessian camp. When he was through, John lay silent with his eyes closed for so long that Christian thought he must have dozed. But when Christian moved to leave, John spoke at last.

"Maybe the thing to do is tell Jacob when he comes home again," he said with a deep sigh.

"But would I be breaking my oath to the king?"

"*Ja.*"

"How can I do that?" demanded Christian. John gazed at him from dark, sunken eyes, and Christian felt the familiar compulsion to tell him everything on the spot — especially about the wound that had led to all this.

"You need to think about this some more," John said slowly, then closed his eyes again. "And so do I. Come back tomorrow. We'll talk about it tomorrow."

"John, there's something else!" Christian blurted, grabbing his friend's arm. John sighed again, but he didn't open his eyes.

"Tomorrow, Christian. Please."

III

The next day, the putrid fever struck. Margaret felt it first, but Charlotte quickly followed, and then Christian succumbed. The fever brought them days on end that felt like dying, but slowly their youth and good health took over.

In less than a week, Frau Volpert found John in a raging chill, as well. For the next three days and nights, she never left the sickroom. Herr Volpert and a weakened Margaret and Christian fetched and carried for her and kept the household going, while little Charlotte stayed downstairs.

As morning broke on the fourth day, Christian tiptoed in with a fresh pitcher of water and some warm corn gruel. Frau Volpert was sagged in a chair by the bed in a rare moment of exhausted sleep. Christian had come to coax some nourishment between John's clenched teeth if he could. The bowl nearly slipped from his hands at John's whisper.

"Christian."

Christian hurried to his bedside and carefully set the bowl on the small table there.

"You're awake," he whispered after a glance toward John's mother. "I'm so glad. How do you feel?"

John offered Christian a hopeless smile. He lifted his hand and as Christian took hold of it, it felt weightless and fragile.

"I want to thank you," John was murmuring.

"I haven't done much," said Christian. "Your mother is the one, really."

"No," answered John with a weak shake of his head. "I mean for everything. For coming to talk to me all this time. You made me feel like I was still alive."

"Of course you're still alive," whispered Christian, alarmed. "You're getting better. You'll be up again in no time, I'm sure of it!"

John withdrew his hand with a gesture of impatience, then grabbed Christian's arm with surprising strength.

"You know, don't you," he said, "that my sister loves you?"

It was a long moment before Christian could answer.

"I think she cares for me," he said slowly, then.

"She loves you," John repeated. He continued in strained urgency. "You could be happy here, Christian. Why go back to Germany? This is a good place for living."

"Yes, John, it is a good place," Christian agreed. He leaned closer to his laboring friend. "Why don't you rest now, and we'll talk a little later."

"No, listen to me," John said, so quietly that Christian could hardly hear. "This is a good country, and its people are fine and brave. Christian . . ."

John stopped and closed his eyes, his hand falling from Christian's arm. Christian bent close, suddenly frightened.

"John," he said. Frau Volpert stirred in her chair. John's eyes fluttered half-open.

"It's a place good enough to die for," whispered John. He turned his head and saw his mother pulling herself straight in her chair. "Mama, I'm thirsty," he said.

He closed his eyes again and lay still. Christian and Frau Volpert stared at him for a moment before the woman said, "Christian, please go and find Herr Volpert for me. Ask him to come up."

The day from that point dragged out in separate minutes. Herr Volpert ran up the stairs by twos and threes. A little later, Margaret was summoned to John's bedside, and then Charlotte, so that finally Christian waited alone downstairs for his own call. Once Margaret came down to fill the water pitcher, but when Christian spoke, she merely shook her head and pressed a hand against her trembling mouth, then quickly remounted the stairs.

At dusk, Christian heard the noise. It was John's mother. She began quietly, but the sound of her voice swelled and rose until the house filled with her wild, keening cry — "John." Christian recoiled in terror at the sound, then ran for the stairs, taking them in leaps as Herr Volpert had earlier. The family was there around the bed, drawing near and closing Christian out. The invitation to bid John farewell had never come, and now it was too late.

IV

Frau Volpert's lament resonated through the anguished days that followed — through the assembling of family and friends, and the formal waiting for burial; through the funeral, at home because the church had been turned into a hospital; and through the interment in the warm, living soil. Her wail became a dirge as family and friends reassembled at the house for the vast meal that was the final concession to formal grief. And when the last mourner had eaten and cried, then taken his leave, John's mother wrapped her vocal grief with her best dishes and stored it away, on the bottom of the stack, so it couldn't fall out and overcome her.

Christian, who had witnessed its full expression, could neither join in her cry nor understand it when she stopped.

He could only roam like a ghost through the weeks of days, numb and vacant with loss.

Then, the day after the burial, he wandered alone into the cowshed, wanting the sound and feel and smell of creatures still living, creatures that gave no thought to death and loneliness. But the sound that carried through the moist, rich air was the last he expected — he heard someone sobbing. In the dim light, Christian made out Margaret standing at the mare's head, stroking and patting the horse's neck exactly as Christian had done on his first day in Reading. All the while, she wept in bare-faced desolation, noticing but not caring when Christian came in.

He hurried along the opposite side of the horse until they stood with only that sleek, undismayed face between them. He reached under and caught Margaret's hand, but no words inspired him. Perhaps it was his silence that released the flood of words from Margaret, as she raised her tear-swollen gaze to him.

"I killed him," she cried. "I killed my brother. I should have known I was sick. I felt terrible and dizzy and odd, but I went to him anyway. I fed him and talked to him when I should have gone away. And now he's dead. John is dead."

A fresh fall of tears streamed down Margaret's face and Christian thought he would drown in them, confused as they suddenly were with the eternal image of John. He'd left before Christian could tell him and be done at last with the nightmare of his own guilt.

An inner voice screamed at Christian to tell Margaret in John's place. She hadn't killed her brother, and Christian could tell her so with conviction. But he had just lost a great piece of the joy that was still so new to him. One friend was dead. To speak now was to risk losing another. Margaret cried on, as Christian did silent battle with himself. In the end, however, he knew that happiness at her expense would simply be the old nightmare with a new twist.

He moved around the horse's head to Margaret's side.

"You didn't kill him," Christian said, no longer touching her. "I did."

She shook her head vehemently.

"I was sick first and I spent much more time with him than you did," she argued.

"He was dying before he ever got the fever, Margaret," he answered. His voice shook from his belly up. "It was the wound that killed him. *I* killed him."

Margaret's crying had slowed and she frowned at her friend.

"I don't understand," she said. "It wasn't your fault he was injured. It was the war."

"Yes, it was my fault," he insisted, a feeling like the putrid fever welling up in him. "I'm the one who did it."

Margaret stared blankly. Then slowly, Christian watched his meaning penetrate. Her eyes widened and dried.

"You!" she cried. "But you never told us!"

"What purpose would it have served?" he asked. After a moment, he added, "I was afraid."

Margaret continued to stare at him. Christian's fears turned his heart to stone as the silence lengthened. At last, he couldn't stand it anymore. He turned and hurried around the mare and out the shed door, through the gate and away down the street, rushing until he was running, and running

135

until he couldn't breathe. Then he walked in long, limping strides, keeping time to his own gasping breaths, shocked at what he had just done.

By the time he reached the Hessian camp, he knew he would have to leave Reading. If Margaret told her parents, he might leave immediately, as a criminal. If she kept his secret, perhaps he'd have time to think, to plan. Either way, he knew he'd lost Margaret. And either way would be the punishment he felt he deserved.

Chapter Eight

I

"I was afraid."

Christian's phrase rang through Margaret's head as she stared at him, hoping she had misunderstood him. But he looked stricken, practically overcome with remorse. She understood him perfectly, after all, and at the same time, she understood herself. She was in love with him — Private Christian Theodor Sigismund Molitor — Hessian soldier, prisoner, enemy.

Christian's eyes begged. Margaret knew she should say something, but her tongue felt numb and no words came, only a chaos of unspoken questions. Not until he turned and raced from the shed did she reach for him past the mare and call his name, too softly, too late. He was gone.

"I was afraid." What did that mean, Margaret wondered? Afraid of what? Punishment? Coward! He wouldn't be blamed for doing his duty. Or would he? Didn't *she* blame him, if truth were told? And what about Mama?

The thought of Mama reined in Margaret's racing thoughts. In fact, her mother certainly would blame Christian, even after all the months of friendship the two men had shared, even knowing that John had grown to love the Hessian, and Christian, John. Margaret could imagine her mother's fury, her demands for blood revenge. Mama must certainly never know.

What purpose would it serve? she thought, and caught herself, shocked. It was an exact echo of Christian's words. And like Christian, she was afraid — afraid of a justice that would be no justice at all.

The mare snorted and tossed her head under Margaret's clutching hand, but Margaret hardly noticed. She must find Christian! The sun hurt her eyes as she pushed wide the shed door and hurried across the yard to the shop. Her father merely shook his head dully; he hadn't seen Christian since breakfast, a fact that didn't touch him in his grief.

Margaret tried the house next, convincing herself that Christian would hardly rush away from her in order to tell his secret to her mother. Mama was nowhere to be seen, but Charlotte sat by the open door, ignoring the pile of mending beside her on the step.

"Mama went to the outlot to pick vegetables," she replied to Margaret's question. She peered at her sister. "Why? What's the matter with you?"

"Nothing," said Margaret. She pulled off her house apron and reached for the sunbonnet hanging by the door. On her

138

way back out, she paused, considered, then asked over her shoulder,

"You haven't seen Christian around, have you, Lottie?"

"Not since he ran out of the gate a little while ago."

"He did!" exclaimed Margaret, spinning to face her. "Did you see which way he went?"

"Sure," said Charlotte. She bent and rummaged among the mending to select a candidate for her darning needle.

"Charlotte!" cried Margaret. She grabbed the younger girl by the chin and raised her face with a jerk. "Don't play games with me! Which way was he heading?"

Charlotte stared at Margaret, her eyes filling with tears.

"Toward the river," she whimpered. She added in a small voice, "Is something wrong? Is Christian in trouble?"

Margaret paused, then patted her sister's cheek softly.

"I don't think so," she said. "I hope not."

She wished, though, that Christian had run in a different direction. The river road also led to the garden lots. Never had that stretch of road seemed so hot or long; but when she arrived, Margaret found only Mama bent over the pea plants.

"Ah," said her mother at Margaret's greeting, "*gut*. I couldn't find you earlier. I can certainly use more hands. But where are your baskets?"

Margaret didn't answer, just squinted off across the long, straight rows of ripening produce — was he one of those distant figures farther along the road?

"Margaret," said Mama. Margaret focused her attention with an effort. "Where *are* your baskets?"

Margaret looked at her own empty hands.

"I guess I forgot them," she said. She started untying her hat strings. "I'll just use my bonnet."

"No," said her mother. "It's too hot to go bare-headed."

Mama rocked back on her heels and peered up at her daughter, leveling a stern look on her.

"Margaret."

"*Ja*, Mama."

"It's time now that the living got on with living."

She held Margaret's gaze as though she might say with her eyes what she would not express in words: *You cannot suffer as I do, but look at me. I go on.* Aloud, she added, "Now, why don't you just work on the weeds while I keep picking. *Ja?*"

"*Ja*, Mama," said Margaret, quickly bending to the task, happy for the concealment of the bonnet. Otherwise, surely, her own eyes would reveal what she would not, *must* not say.

II

The morning in the sun dragged, and the walk home seemed endless. Margaret watched every distant walker down the road or in the fields, half-expecting to be overtaken by a returning Christian. When the midday meal was served and Christian still didn't appear, Margaret could hardly manage the food on her plate. Where could he be?

"You've given him too much freedom," Mama complained. "He thinks he's one of us and can do as he pleases. My own children don't take such liberties!"

"Anna, you forget yourself," Papa said quietly. "The boy is beside himself. He must have loved our Johnny well."

Mama stopped in the middle of removing Christian's unused plate from the table, and the hard line of her mouth eased. At the sight of her mother's softened expression, Margaret prayed silently.

Please let me talk to him first when he comes home. Then her ongoing worry took a new shape and she added, *But first, please let him come home.*

By supper that evening, everyone was on edge. Papa said little but his attention was often directed to the door or out the window. At one point, he suddenly rose and hurried to the porch. He even took a quick turn to the workshop and back, before he returned to his meal.

"Thought I heard something," he explained to his silently watching family. "I was afraid the mare was loose."

By true nightfall, the knock at the back door brought the whole family to their feet.

Papa cleared his throat and went with measured leisure to answer, while Margaret and her mother exchanged sheepish looks and sat back down.

"Oh, it's you. *Guten Abend,*" he said.

George Scheffer stepped past him, extending a general greeting before he turned to Mama.

"I'm sorry, Frau Volpert," he said. "I don't mean to intrude. Actually, I was looking for Molitor. I wanted to see him about my boot. His repair hasn't lasted, as you can see."

He lifted the boot he carried, its sole flapping loose at the toe.

"I'm sorry, too, George," she answered calmly. "Christian is not here just now. He's out on an errand for me."

"You're welcome to wait," added her husband. "But he'll probably be quite late."

"I'll tell him about your boot," contributed Charlotte.

Margaret stared in amazement at her family. In that moment, they had closed ranks around Christian as though he were a Volpert. George's smile flattened and his eyes narrowed as he looked intently from one to another of them, his gaze resting finally on Margaret. She hastily bent to the needlework in her lap.

"I see," he said at last. "I'll just come back another time. No hurry — it was warm for sitting inside, so I thought I'd stroll." With that, he nodded and left.

No one spoke. From outside came the squeak and clack of the front gate, then nothing but the sound of cicadas and crickets, matched in counterpoint to one another. Papa and Mama settled silently to the small tasks George had interrupted, and their daughters did the same. After a half-dozen stitches, however, Margaret laid her work aside and stood, stretching her arms above her head.

"It *is* a warm night," she said. "I think I'll step outside for a breath before bed."

The faintest breeze stirred through the yard, rustling the maple's thick growth of leaves. Margaret moved from the house to put herself more in the way of the soft current, listening all the while for approaching footsteps in the lane beyond the front gate. Her memory was full of that other night when George had been out here. Did he really leave just now? She crossed to the workshop, staring at the dark windows. Suddenly that darkness turned a deeper midnight! Some faint light had just been extinguished!

Christian? she wondered and started for the door. But caution and memory held her back, and a moment later, the door was opened.

As the figure emerged into the open yard, Margaret recognized the shape and set of George. He stopped a moment, appearing to listen, then crossed the yard. Without a sound, he leaped over the gate; and at the same moment, something caught a bit of light as it fell to the ground behind him.

When Margaret was sure he was gone she walked thoughtfully to the path and bent to see what George had dropped. She was patting the ground for it in the soft shadows when she heard her father's voice.

"Margaret? Are you there?"

"*Ja*, Papa," she called.

"Are you all right, child?" he asked.

"*Ja*, Papa," she repeated. "I'll be in shortly."

"We're going to bed," he said. "Will you snuff the light when you come in?"

"*Ja*, Papa."

"Margaret?"

"*Ja?*"

"We'll go out and find him if he's still gone in the morning. You needn't worry."

"I won't be long, Papa. You go ahead to bed."

The silhouette drew back from the doorway. Margaret waited a beat, then felt again for whatever had fallen. Almost immediately, her hand brushed against the hard edges of a folded parchment. She turned back to the kitchen with it, but then hesitated. On second thought, she carried it instead to the workshop, carefully feeling her way in and to the table under the window where the tin lamp and flint were kept. Her hands shook as she lit the lamp, then hastily lowered it to the floor, and shaded it on all but one side. Kneeling beside it, she smoothed the paper flat on the floor where the light shone.

The first words she deciphered were names — her father's in the greeting at the top of the paper, Christian's signed at the bottom, and her own in the last sentence. In fact, what George had dropped was a letter. *What was he doing with such a letter? Had he stolen it?* Perhaps it held some clue to George's behavior, and to the whole mysterious day. So she set about reading the words one by one, drawing desperately on her scant training in letters.

The labor was painfully slow, but finally, she worked her way through to Christian's signature. Now she knew. But what should she do about it? Her action could change her life — and maybe the future of the war!

III

Even as Margaret read his letter, Christian raced across the moonlit Pennsylvania countryside on a stolen horse, his thoughts ranging over the tangled events of the day.

His flight to the Hessian camp that morning had been an act of sheer impulse. There was nothing and no one for him at the camp. By the time he reached it, he felt convinced there was nothing and no one for him anywhere.

He had rambled among the trees, past tents and small gardens, keeping to himself and fighting off the waves of panic and loneliness that made his knees shake and his heart pound.

Then from some distance off, he had heard his name called. He looked ahead and saw Hans Guber. Without stopping to think what he was doing, Christian veered off into a denser grove of evergreens and walked steadily away from the friendly Hessian, down a steep hill and right to the banks of the Schuylkill River.

Sight of Hans had brought a great flood of memories to Christian's mind, memories of a morning's conversation with Hans and two other prisoners — was it only two weeks ago? Christian had wondered then what to do with the information the Hessians unwittingly handed him. He had asked John for help, but John had left him too soon.

Why did you leave me, John, Christian cried silently. *I don't know what to do!*

As he stood staring out over the river, he had thought of George offering to carry information to the British. Christian had resisted him without fully understanding why. But there by the river, an idea began to form. As it grew and took shape, it shone like a shaft of light into the dark confusion that had threatened to overwhelm Christian since the day John died.

At last, he had known what to do. No longer would he flounder between his own past and this new world of ideas and possibilities opened to him. He had turned then from the river and continued north to the hills and the roundabout route back into Reading.

Riding on through the night, Christian remembered how

endless the day had seemed. First scouting through town for a horse, and then a weapon that would be easily pilfered later. Long before day's end, he had nothing left to do but wait while his imagination ran wild and his nerves stretched taut.

The worst moment came when he let himself into the Volpert dooryard. He could hear the family clearly at supper through the open door. He heard Margaret mention his name, and faltered, wondering with a deep pang whether he could follow his chosen course, after all. The sound of her voice so befuddled him that he walked into the water trough with a thud. He barely made it through the shop door before he heard Herr Volpert in the yard. The older man went so far as to push open the shop door and quietly call Christian's name. Christian didn't move, didn't breathe. After listening a moment, Herr Volpert left, shutting the door behind him, and leaving Christian free to do what he'd come to do.

He had few belongings, just a change of clothes that he rolled up in his light blanket and fastened with a piece of rope. For the first time since Brandywine, he remembered the beautiful leather pack his father had given him. It hadn't traveled to the hospital with Christian; had it been buried instead among the devastated American army? Like his past?

Christian took a final look around the loft in the dusty light from the window. At the last minute, he moved to the washstand and felt around behind the water basin. He pulled out three small items. One was a linen handkerchief Charlotte had given him as a surprise. It was embroidered with a C. "For Christian," she had said as she kissed his cheek and giggled. "Or Charlotte," she added in innocent coquetry.

Christian pocketed the gift with a sigh. The next object was a gold coin that John had given him shortly before he died.

"General Washington himself awarded me that," he'd said, "for rum, after the Battle of Trenton. But I couldn't bring myself to drink it away."

When Christian tried to refuse the gift, John wouldn't hear of it.

"Keep it," he said. "It'll remind you of the kind of men who believe we have a right to be free."

John had made a hole in the coin to wear it around his neck on a leather string. Christian unknotted the string and pulled it out. In its place, he threaded the third and final object, a silky blue ribbon that had flown from Margaret's tied-back hair one windy day while they were riding in the wagon. Christian found it later, lodged in the back among some empty barrels, and kept it. The ribbon seemed to carry the spirit of the young woman who had worn it, and he knotted it and placed it around his neck, where the weight of John's coin pulled it tight.

Once more below in the shop, Christian had bent with borrowed quill and paper to write his letter, a job as tedious to him as was the reading of it later for Margaret.

> *Dear Herr Volpert,*
> *I apologize for my poor manners in not speaking to you face to face before I leave. But I know something that could change the outcome of the war and I was afraid you might try to stop me.*

*Please understand that as long as I live, if
I live, I will remember you and your family
with fondness and gratitude. Please convey to
Frau Volpert my thanks, and to the little one, my
special regards.*

*And now, I can wait no longer. I know what
I have to do. No matter what happens, I won't
return to Reading. Margaret knows why. I hope
she will forgive me someday.*

> *Auf Wiedersehen,*
> *Christian Theodor Sigismund Molitor*

Christian propped his letter conspicuously against a big
boot on Herr Volpert's workbench, then threw his blanket
roll out the small back window of the shop that faced away
from the house, and squeezed through after it. Once free of
the building, he crouched away through the shrubbery to
the open lane.

Now, remembering all this with miles between him and
Reading, Christian's heart pounded painfully. The gallop-
ing motion of the horse pulled the blue ribbon against his
neck again and again, and he reached his hand up to hold
John's coin.

IV

Margaret read Christian's letter more easily the second time,
and as she did, a terrible sense of helpless loneliness came
over her. She couldn't imagine what he might know that
"could change the outcome of the war" or how he'd come

upon the information. Did it have anything to do with George Scheffer and his mysterious visits? He was looking for Christian tonight. He found the letter, and meant to carry it off. Why?

Margaret stared intently into the lantern flame, wishing she could smooth out and decipher her memories and impressions the way she had Christian's letter. She remembered Jacob's doubts about his friend when George chose army-exempt work over enlistment. She remembered the day George had rescued her from the British officer, with English rolling off his tongue in an astonishing way. She thought of the time she'd found George with Christian, and of the conversation she had overheard between them. Then there was his skulking tonight. Was Jacob right? Was George a Loyalist?

Margaret quickly grabbed the letter and blew out the light, bent on rousing her father to the rescue. Somehow, Christian had found important information. He would almost certainly seek out Jacob at Sandy Beach to deliver it to the American army. He would have no way of knowing George had found his letter nor how dreadfully angry George always became when he was thwarted in anything. Margaret had left the shop, crossed the yard, and let herself into the kitchen before a new fear occurred to her and stopped her cold.

What if Christian was actually on his way to the British? Margaret shook her head vigorously. The one thing she had to believe was that Christian was no spy. He was honorable, she would stake her life on it. Above all else, Christian had to be warned about George.

But suppose her father didn't believe her scanty evidence against George, and so refused to go on a "wild goose chase." Or worse yet, suppose Papa didn't believe in Christian's good intentions. The letter was ambiguous. He might call the militia to go after *Christian*. Not only would Christian's information be lost to General Washington, but Christian could be tried and hanged as a spy!

"Margaret?" came Papa's voice from the front room. Margaret swallowed hard against the tightening in her throat.

"Yes, Papa, it's me," she called. "I'm dousing the light now. Good night."

"Any sign of Christian?" he asked.

"No," she answered, hiding the letter in the folds of her skirt, in case he came out to the kitchen. "Good night."

But he didn't appear, merely called "good night." He sounded terribly weary and for a moment Margaret reconsidered. Finally, though, she simply couldn't take the chance of being frustrated in helping her friend. She blew out the candle, and ascended to her room.

A quarter of an hour's silent activity readied Margaret. While she changed into a heavier skirt and boots, her mind raced, making and rejecting one plan after another. How could she stop George herself; or if he was already chasing Christian, how could she catch up with him? Or find and warn Christian? She was a town girl, with scant experience at either handling the wagon or riding alone. She didn't even know how to find Christian or the way to Sandy Beach, assuming that was where he'd gone. Even as she tiptoed back downstairs, expertly avoiding all the creaks and loose boards, she knew she might be making a disastrous mistake.

150

It didn't matter. George must be prevented from finding Christian.

Margaret made a fast walk of the two dark blocks to the Scheffer house. Light spilled out the cracked-open stable door as she hurried across their yard. She could see nothing through the crack, so she slowly, carefully pulled on the door. Without warning, it gave a loud resisting ratch.

"Who's there?" demanded George. He spun around from strapping a saddle pack to his horse and stared into the dark doorway. He was dressed for riding, his hair tied back, his boots on. Margaret stepped into the lighted space. "Margaret!"

George loomed over her, his very posture a violent threat. Her heart beat so hard she wasn't sure she could speak. Her fears had all been justified. Now she must make her plan work. She took a deep breath and the words began to spill out of her mouth, as she had practiced them on the way.

"Oh George, thank goodness I've found you!" she cried. "I don't know what to do. Christian has run away. He's been gone since morning and I'm sure he's on his way back to the British. I could tell you suspected something at our house, and I wanted to say something, but I couldn't. Mama and Papa have no idea. I'm the only one who knows. He's going because of something I said, and he's going to do something terrible. I've got to stop him!"

She paused, trying to interpret George's expression, but he was characteristically unreadable. She laid a tentative hand on his sleeve. "George, I need your help. Will you help me? Please?"

George was silent a moment before he answered. His gaze never left Margaret's face.

"What terrible thing do you think he's doing?" he asked finally.

"Betraying us!" she cried. George's eyes flared open.

"How could Christian do that?" he asked.

"When Jacob was home, he spoke alone with John and Christian for a while. He told me later he had mentioned a confidential matter and was worried about it."

"Why would Christian wait until now? Jacob was in Reading two weeks ago," George asked.

"I don't think he intended to tell. And there was the funeral and all," said Margaret. She lowered her voice with unfeigned sorrow. John's memory gave her sudden new boldness. "But this morning, I made him awfully angry. That's when he left."

"Do you know where he's gone?" he asked. A faint smile altered the shape of his mouth. "The British aren't all in one place."

"Well, I can't be sure, of course," she said slowly. *Careful, now*, she thought. *There's no turning back.* "But I suppose he would look for the man in charge, wouldn't he? General Clinton?"

"That makes sense," George answered slowly.

"Will you help me then?" she asked.

"How?" asked George.

"Take me to find him," she said. "Help me catch him before he gets to the British."

For a split second George looked stunned.

"Take you . . ." he started. He threw his head back and laughed harshly. Then he stopped abruptly and looked

Margaret up and down, taking in her town skirt and sturdy shoes and the tight braid of her hair down her back. He looked her straight in the eye. "Margaret, do you know what you're saying? It would take us three days hard riding if we didn't find him short of Wa— . . . Clinton's headquarters. You'd be alone with me, day and night. Do you understand the kind of trouble you would be in?"

Margaret swallowed nervously.

"*Ja*," asserted Margaret with conviction born of near panic.

"You'd better go home before you're missed and let me handle it," George was saying. "I'll find him and bring him back, if I can."

"No!" cried Margaret and suspicion narrowed George's eyes. She hastily added, "Actually, there's something I haven't told you."

She waited for George to say something. Instead, he simply stood, folding his arms across his chest and watching her closely.

"You see," she continued carefully, "before we . . . argued, Christian said something odd. He said, 'I know two things, Margaret, and either one of them could make a difference in this war.' "

George's attention was riveted to Margaret's face with such intensity that she felt he must be able to read her thoughts. With a last desperate effort, she went on.

"Then he said, 'The amazing part is, one thing could give the Americans the edge, while the other could help the British wipe out the Continental Army!' " Margaret mustered every ounce of her self-control. She could tell that the hook was in George's mouth — she had to make him swallow! "If you take me along, I might be able to get him to go to General Washington, instead of General Clinton. If you won't, I'll have to tell my father, and we'll *both* go with you. That would be proper, wouldn't it? I'm just afraid it'll waste too much time."

George's eyes seemed to be staring at some far distant object.

"Christian might at least be willing to tell *you* what he knows," he murmured thoughtfully. His face assumed a pious expression. "So that you and I can tell Washington, if he won't. All right, Margaret, I'll do it. But it has to be just the two of us. You're right. We can't waste a minute."

George moved closer to her, and put his arm around her shoulders.

"Now listen," he said. "I'll tell you what we have to do."

While George proceeded to outline a plan of action, Margaret gave herself over to her own plans, fighting the revulsion she suddenly felt at George's nearness.

"What did you say to Christian, anyway, to make him so angry?" George asked, when at last they were adjusting the saddle and packs to accommodate two riders.

Margaret opened her mouth but nothing came out. She quickly lowered her head, frantically trying to think of something, anything, that would sound plausible. But it was George himself who saved her.

"Did he want something you wouldn't give him?" he asked quietly.

Margaret closed her eyes in a quick prayer of thanksgiving

and nodded wordlessly. She felt George's hand under her chin and raised her face. She was close to tears by now, but whatever George saw seemed only to bolster his confidence.

"Never mind," he said with a disconcerting smile. "I'll help you. Let's go."

Chapter Nine

I

Christian rode on through the darkened hills, pushing east and north, anxious to get as far as possible before daybreak. He had only a general idea of the way after Bethlehem, but just to get that far seemed challenge enough.

Christian rode through most of the night, with only a short pre-dawn nap. He stopped to rest his horse and collect orchard windfalls, but not until evening was settling once again did he consider sleeping. Even then, he pushed on, determined to go as far as possible in the least amount of time. A steady drizzling rain soaked his clothes, adding to his weariness with the weight it added. Finally, in the first still hours after midnight, he gave in to the urge to sleep. He firmly tethered his animal and made his bed on the soft forest ground. In his last waking moments, he wondered how far he'd come and what Herr Volpert had thought of his letter.

* * *

"Hey, mister," piped a young voice. "Are you all right?"

Christian came abruptly awake, his eyes opened wide. He lay on his back, staring up into the face of a young boy who returned his gaze with dark unblinking eyes.

"You're not sick or anything, are you?" the child asked in the Americanized German so familiar to Christian.

The boy was soaked with rain but he didn't seem to notice, merely shifted rhythmically from one bare foot to the other, waiting, while water dripped off the blunt end of his nose. As Christian pushed himself up to a sitting position, he discovered that he, too, was drenched to the skin, because he lay in a large puddle. He had raised himself to his feet when he heard bells ringing.

"What's that!?" demanded Christian. "Is it a warning?"

"*Nein*," answered the boy. "It's Sunday. The bells always ring on Sunday."

"Sunday," repeated Christian. He shook his head to clear it and a fine spray of water flew around him. "Of course."

The boy nodded and smiled, then turned as though to leave.

"Wait!" cried Christian. The child turned back. "What time is it?"

"Just past the midday, mister," he answered. "I gotta get home."

"Where's home?" asked Christian, as he gathered up his wet belongings.

"Down there," the boy said and gestured over his shoulder with his thumb. All Christian could see in that direction

157

was his mare grazing at her tether, and more woodland.

"Is it a town?" he asked.

"Yes," said the child, looking surprised. "What do you think?"

"What's its name?" Christian asked. The boy gazed at him warily, and said nothing. Christian dug in his pants pocket for a penny. "Here," he continued and extended it toward the child. "This is yours if you'll tell me where I am and take me to the closest tavern."

The boy's eyes brightened at sight of the penny.

"It's Bethlehem, mister," he said eagerly, taking the coin and stowing it quickly away. "There's only one inn. Can I ride on the horse?"

"We both will," Christian agreed.

Soon, the horse with its riders was descending into Bethlehem by a trail just north of the main road. Christian remembered well his last sight of the town, as he had ridden away with Herr Volpert in the wagon, war-lame and frightened by this strange new world with its rebellious citizens. As the horse left the narrow path for a broader lane leading into the heart of Bethlehem, Christian shook his head. How great a distance he had come in the ensuing two years. The voyage to America was short by comparison.

The boy, plucking at his sleeve, brought Christian out of his reverie.

"You turn here," he said and pointed. A half block after the turn, the horse came alongside a tavern bustling with activity. As Christian reined in, the child slid to the ground and bolted. He disappeared around a corner so fast Christian had no time even to thank him.

Inside, the tavern's bustle suited Christian well. The tavern keeper hardly noticed him as he asked for the best route to the "Highlands," one of Jacob's few name references to the present battle lines.

"Well, those hills cover some territory," the man said. He carried a pair of empty tankards in one hand and pulled at his long whiskers with the other. "But if you head on to Easton and ferry the Delaware there, you can follow the route north from Phillipsburg on the other side."

As he spoke, the taverner waved the tankards this way and that; and instead of making his explanation clearer, he was confusing Christian all the more. To make matters worse, the aroma of roast fowl and fresh pork was stirring Christian's stomach juices to a distracting degree.

"The road runs up through Oxford and Wallpack to Sussex," finished the man. "That'll put you where you want to be."

Someone on the other side of the room called for service and he excused himself, leaving Christian befuddled and famished. He closed his eyes and concentrated on the town names the tavern keeper had listed, committing them to memory in a sort of rhythmic litany until his hunger would be ignored no longer. He had precious few coppers, but he knew he must revive himself and his horse.

So it was another half hour before he resumed his mission, bolstered with ale, dark bread, and a windfall apple from his saddlebag, and with his horse well-oated. He ventured now into territory he had never before traveled, and he rode on a fresh wave of loneliness that he began to think would accompany him forever.

II

As Christian fought his loneliness, Margaret, with George, had all the company she could handle. The first time she managed to loosen a pouch from the saddlebag and let it drop, he stopped, annoyed but willing to retrieve it. The next time, he reined in with an angry exclamation in English and barely gave Margaret time to pick it up and remount. When she tried it again, George pulled the horse up so hard and fast that they were nearly thrown. George turned to look at the bedroll where it lay, then at Margaret behind him, his breathing quick and noisy. Then he faced front again and kicked the horse into motion, leaving the blanket where it had fallen.

Only once did Margaret pretend a faint in the saddle that nearly landed her under the horse's hooves. George rode like a man obsessed. She could imagine that he would have left her, like the bedroll, if she had fallen. He would allow nothing to slow their pace. By the first daybreak, when Margaret thought she really would collapse, George stopped at a wayside house only long enough to feed the horse. Before she knew it, he was shaking her awake on the bench where she dozed.

"Here," he said, and handed her a warm cheese pasty and a mug of fresh milk. "The woman inside sold me some fine-looking meat pies for later. So eat up! We can't dawdle."

Margaret started with a small bite, but she was too hungry to eat slowly. In no time they were back in the saddle. During the worst heat of midday, they dozed under the roadside trees for no more than two hours before George pulled her up in the saddle once again. She had long since given up riding pillion, and now straddled the horse just like her companion, with her skirt tucked around her legs, sore and aching as never before in her life.

Into the evening they rode, with George rationing out food as they went, and frustrating Margaret's plans at every turn. Finally, when the road was dark as pitch, she spoke in his ear.

"If we don't stop, I'm going to be terribly sick," she said and paused, but George made no acknowledgment. "I mean it, George."

She felt the horse check its fast walk, which was the best pace George could manage in the dark, even with the lantern he carried. George spoke over his shoulder.

"Maybe I should find some farm or inn to leave you," he said, his voice stretched with impatience. "This is too much for you, Margaret."

"You can't keep this up, either!" she cried. "Not without some sleep! Can't we stop at the next tavern and *really* rest?"

George was silent for a moment.

"Very well," he said then with a sigh. He added in a tone like flint, "but if you aren't ready to move on when I say so, you stay behind. Understood?"

"*Ja,*" she answered.

It was heaven to fall onto the eiderdown mattress. Margaret never noticed or cared about the other women travelers in the room with her. She hadn't been this tired since the night she'd nursed Christian in the Moravian hospital, and it was on this thought that she fell deeply, dreamlessly asleep.

The innkeeper's wife wakened her with difficulty.

"Your brother is ready to leave," she whispered. Margaret could barely force her eyes open and could see nothing when she did. It took a long moment to remember and focus. Her brother, the woman said. Margaret sighed as she remembered the fiction under which she and George were traveling.

"It's still night," she protested.

" 'S almost day," answered the woman. "I been up some already."

They traveled through rain all morning, but it slowed to a misting by the time they reached Bethlehem. Riding along those familiar streets, Margaret hung to George's waist in dripping, frightened weariness. George had been unnervingly quiet since her shoe "accidentally" fell off her foot, forcing one more stop.

"We'll stop here for supper," he announced at the Bethlehem inn. The sound of his voice startled her after his long silence.

"And some sleep?" she asked as she slid off the horse, but he didn't answer.

As they ate and drank, George watched the inn's other occupants, the predictable mix of locals and travelers, and he kept a sharp eye on the door when anyone entered.

"George," Margaret began once. He met her gaze with a flat expression that held much but gave nothing away. She had seen the same look that morning when she said she needed to stop "for private reasons," her most effective device. He had stopped. But as she landed at the horse's side and glanced up, he was staring down at her in just this disconcerting way.

"Margaret," he had said quietly. "For someone who was in

such urgent need of help, you're being incredibly bothersome. If I didn't know better, I'd say you don't really want to find Molitor."

Margaret's mouth had gone dry at his tone then, and it went dry now. She cleared her throat and lifted a forkful of the mutton from her plate.

"Tasty," she said and stuck it in her mouth with a forced smile.

Immediately after supper, George moved to leave and Margaret followed with dragging steps, all but done in. When they left Bethlehem, she left all that was familiar to her. By George's account, the next milestone was the Delaware River, and for the first time, she considered giving up. Suddenly, she wanted to make him take her back to Bethlehem, to the hospital or the Widows' House where she certainly could find shelter. But even as she thought it, her opportunity had already slipped away. By dark, they would reach the river and the ferry to New Jersey.

Dusk came early in the rain, along the wooded road to Easton. By the time they neared the end of the ten-mile trek, the horse was slipping on the muddy road, making the welcomed lights of Easton dance before Margaret's weary eyes. When George pushed on through the town to the river crossing, Margaret bit back her objections. The same sense of caution that had served her in the past was vibrating within her, *carefully, carefully*.

George raised his lantern as they rode beyond the last building on the edge of town. In its light, Margaret could see the miry roadbed begin to slope away.

"Just down the hill after Maguire's old place," the blacksmith had said, when George stopped to ask. "The ferryman has a house off to the left when you reach the river."

They slowed so the horse wouldn't lose its footing. The ferryman's gate was easy to spot, with a brightly lit lamp on a post with a sign.

"You stay here with the horse," George said and dismounted.

Margaret obeyed wordlessly. As George moved away with his small lantern, she looked off at the lighter dark where the river must be, then realized that another lantern bobbed there. As she watched, the ferry itself became visible, with several figures on it. Margaret nudged the horse forward, closing the distance between the gate and the wharf.

The ferry raft had just moved off its mooring, and she could see the man pushing the long pole into the dark water. A horse was swimming on a lead behind, and the lantern's glow caught at least one other figure. A creeping sensation started at the nape of Margaret's scalp and made her skin tingle. She knew that second form, those clothes. She'd mended the breeches only a week ago. Disbelief was quickly supplanted by horror.

Margaret heard a door slam, then the sound of splashing, running footsteps. She heard George's voice, and her name, followed by a string of oaths. At the wharfside, he grabbed her by the forearm and dragged her off the horse. When she fell he pulled her roughly to her feet and swore again.

"What do you think you're doing?" he growled. Margaret's knees hardly supported her. She tried to speak, but a whimper was all that came out.

"Why didn't you wait for me?" George raged. "We have to catch the last run!"

"That's it," she said breathlessly.

"What's it?" George demanded.

"The ferry," she answered, exerting the last of her courage. "I saw it going. I was trying to stop it, but I was too late."

"What? Gone?" George spun toward the river and Margaret stopped breathing. Had the boat moved far enough away? Could he see the passenger? George exploded in a fresh blast of curses.

"Well, that's that, then," he said at last. Margaret sagged against the horse with a silent sigh. "We're stuck here for the night — the woman said he's staying over there till morning. So you'll get the blasted sleep you've been moaning about. Enjoy it. It's the last you get until we find that bastard, Molitor!"

They returned to the ferryman's house, and the man's wife gave them what they needed in refreshment and quarters. Yet for all her exhaustion, Margaret waited hours for sleep. Her mind cast back and forth between that shadowy figure of Christian — *surely* it was Christian — on the ferry, and the memory of George's bruising anger at the wharf. One thing was clear — her next effort to stop George would have to be ruthless, because it would certainly be her last chance, whatever the outcome.

III

In the first light, they were off again, and George drove them tirelessly as soon as they touched the New Jersey shore at Phillipsburg. They struck off to the north and rode straight through the heat of the day, with no rain this time to either slow them down or cool them off. All the time, thinking furiously, Margaret watched the road ahead.

George no longer heeded Margaret's requests for stops. They stopped only when he needed to stop. During the brief rest in Oxford, George insisted that Margaret stay with him rather than wait inside the stable where they fed the horse. He spoke to the hostler in English, the German-Americans having been left behind on the Pennsylvania side of the river. When the man was gone, Margaret asked for a translation. George glanced at her briefly, then continued saddling up with a shrug.

"He was just saying that the next stretch is a little forsaken," said George. His voice jerked with his vigorous strapping and tightening of the horse's gear. "He thought we should go forewarned . . . maybe carry extra food . . . and a weapon."

"Do we have extra food?" she asked, her mind racing.

"We will soon," answered George, with a last tug at the strap.

"Do we have a weapon?" Margaret asked.

George hoisted himself into the saddle and turned to her with his hand outstretched. He wore that flat, impassive expression again.

"Of course," he said and pulled her up behind him.

The road they traveled turned between enormous outcroppings of rock on one side and dense woods on the other, the going rough and stony. And just as they came slowly into a straightaway, Margaret thought she saw another horse, rounding a bend ahead of them. She couldn't be sure — George didn't seem to notice anything — but her immediate impression was overpowering. It must be Christian! Just before the bend was a small crossroads with a clearing on the wooded side of the road.

"George," she said. "Please, stop. Just a minute, I promise. But I *have* to stop."

Surprisingly, George pulled up, maybe because of the urgency in her voice, and they both dismounted. Margaret dashed off into the underbrush, then waited, taking as much time as she thought she could. When she returned to the clearing she made a show of hurrying. George was preparing to remount, and she moved to do the same, then turned to him as though on impulse.

"Do you want to use the woods, too?" she asked timidly. She glanced nervously around them and added. "Only don't go far. And hurry!"

George looked from her to the woods to the horse, then up into the westering sunlight. His unshaven face looked all the more travel worn and menacing in the afternoon light. Why had she never before noticed how big he was?

"All right," he said, after a moment. He anchored the reins with a rock, while Margaret bent and stretched. She kept it up as he walked away, fully prepared for his backward glance when it came. After he had moved out of sight, she waited one beat longer. Then she flew to the horse, threw the reins over its head, and got her foot into the stirrup.

Twice, she tried to mount without success. The horse's movement and Margaret's skirt kept her from flinging her leg over its breadth quickly enough. She took a deep breath to quell her growing panic, bunched her skirt into her right hand, and threw herself with all her terrified strength one more time, up and into the saddle.

By sheer instinct, she turned the animal and gave it a vicious kick in the ribs. In that moment, the world went wild; a deafening roar thundered in her ear and the horse threw itself violently upward, bolting right out from under her. Margaret hit the ground with a numbing thwack that jarred every bone, joint, and tooth.

Her vision hadn't cleared when she was dragged to her feet so roughly that she screamed in pain.

George had her by one arm and was hurling words of abuse at her so rapidly she couldn't make out where one word ended and the next began. He waved a pistol over her head like a crazy man, and when he ran out of insults he raised it and brought it brutally down to hit her. At the last instant, she jerked her free arm up to protect herself and immediately heard the sound of cracking bone and her own scream. The world exploded into swirling black, shot through with flashing light.

IV

Until he crossed the Delaware, Christian had traveled with half his mind looking over his shoulder. Even as the ferry took him across, he thought he heard someone calling, "Margaret!" from the Pennsylvania shore. But when he looked back, all was dark at the wharf, and he decided his mind played cruel tricks on him.

Once on the opposite shore, however, a new confidence welled up in him, and with it new energy. This countryside was strange to him and carried neither memories nor threats. By noon, he was through Oxford, riding the most rugged road he had traveled so far, on a wave of hope.

Not until midafternoon did Christian see signs of human life. The sun burned hot where the town had pushed back the forest's shade, and Christian could find few citizens out of doors in it, certainly no one who spoke German. Finally, a merchant sitting outside his shop offered assistance. With gestures and single syllables, they achieved a conversation of sorts.

Christian mentally checked off the list of towns he had heard from the innkeeper. Easton and Phillipsburg had flanked his river crossing. He had supped at noon in Oxford. What was next. Velpeck? Or was it Vallpeck?

The merchant was frowning over Christian's pronunciation, when a passing woman stopped and suggested,

"Wallpack? Are you asking for Wallpack?"

Christian nodded eagerly. He gestured to the town around them and repeated the name. The man and woman exchanged a short gabble and a laugh, then shook their heads.

"This is Changewater, lad," said the man. *Changewater!* thought Christian. *That wasn't one of the towns the innkeeper mentioned. I must have missed my turning somewhere.*

The helpful pair were engaged, by now, in a confusing disagreement, while Christian concentrated furiously on their directions. It appeared that both roads leading north from town eventually arrived in Wallpack, and neither one was clearly preferable. Finally, Christian decided to choose on a whim, and he bade the pair a friendly farewell. But they had become too involved in their argument to notice.

Christian was still a half-mile short of the crossroads when the shot, and then the scream, ripped through the quiet forest like a blade through canvas.

His horse bolted forward in surprise, but Christian reined in and listened. He could hear nothing now but the rustle and sigh of the woods that surrounded him, and the nervous snorts of the mare. He drew his stolen pistol and coaxed the horse forward again, rounding each bend and cresting every hill with all the caution of a trained soldier.

When the crossroads came into view, he stopped and listened again. Now he heard voices and proceeded slowly.

The clearing came in sight. A woman lay on the ground, hugging herself and weeping. Beside her paced a man, swearing in German and alternately waving his handgun in wild arcs and pointing it at the woman. She seemed not to care, only wept on.

At that moment, just as Christian's mind made the impossible identification of the actors in the scene before him, they saw him.

"No-o-o-oo!" the woman screamed.

George swooped down behind Margaret and pulled her up against him tightly, making her a human shield.

"A-a-a-ah, my arm!" wailed Margaret. Then she cried out, "Run, Christian! He'll kill you!"

"You move, turncoat, and I kill your girl," cried George. He turned the pistol until it pointed at Margaret's head. "Throw your gun away."

Christian's gun hand held steady. After the first glance at Margaret, he looked only at George. *Concentrate!* he commanded himself.

"You've got me wrong," he said aloud to George.

George moved the gun's muzzle until it was actually touching her head.

"Now!" he yelled.

Christian slowly tossed his weapon off to one side.

"You know something," George continued. "Something for the rebels. Something for us. You tell me, now, or she's dead."

Christian straightened.

"Forget the girl," he said. "Why hang yourself? You and I are on the same side. Let her go, and then we can talk."

George swore and pushed the gun harder against Margaret's head so that she whimpered.

"Liar!" he yelled. "Talk or I kill her. And then I'll kill you."

Christian looked from Margaret's white, clenched face to George's.

"You'll be murdering a friend," said Christian.

"I'll be a hero for the crown, turncoat," George spat. "She and all the rest of you chose other friends a long time ago. Now talk!"

"Don't!" cried Margaret.

Christian stared at the weapon. He looked George directly in the eye, and saw the venomous intensity there. His gaze shifted again to Margaret's pleading eyes.

"I can't let him kill you, Margaret," he said.

"Sweet," sneered George.

Christian talked. He told of Stony Point's weakness; then he went on to tell about the secret troops stationed upriver of the vulnerable fort. As he spoke, Margaret closed her eyes and began again to weep, only now it was as though her heart was broken, and not her arm. And all the while, Christian was inching, ever so carefully, closer to her and her captor.

Christian modulated his voice as he spoke, self-consciously mimicking the cadence of Margaret's soothing sickroom conversations. He waited to see George's attention finally shift from Christian himself to what he was' saying. And when the moment came, Christian used it as the only weapon he had left. He screamed and pointed behind George. As George whipped around, Christian lunged and shoved Margaret away, then tackled George. With the two men locked against each other, rolling and struggling on the ground with the gun between them, the whole meaning of life was reduced to a furious contest over possession of that instrument of death.

When the shot blasted the still afternoon air, time itself seemed to stop to discover the winner.

"Christian?" Margaret quavered nearby.

Christian barely heard her through the reverberations of the gun's discharge. He could feel the weapon's cold shape in his hand. He pulled on it tentatively. George didn't resist. Instead, he seemed to lean back and roll away. Christian waited, poised for George's next move.

"Christian!" Margaret repeated sharply.

172

He reached out and put his hand against George's chest. There was no rise and fall, no betraying rhythm of life, and when Christian removed his hand, he saw George's blood on it.

"I'm all right, Margaret," Christian answered.

V

"So George agreed to bring me along," Margaret explained later while Christian finished making a sling for her arm. "I didn't know what else I could do. I thought you were going to Jacob at Sandy Beach."

Christian's ministrations came to a momentary halt. He resumed with exaggerated care, keeping his eyes on his work.

"*Ja?* You thought I was going to Jacob?" he asked quietly. "And what do you think now?"

"Well, I . . . you said, I mean," stammered Margaret. Then she lapsed into silence, and she could feel the warmth flooding her face. "Oh Christian, I'm sorry. You were going to Sandy Beach, weren't you!"

Christian simply smiled in a way that offered her another chance.

"Of course," she said gratefully. "Christian, why did you come back?"

"What do you mean, 'back'?" he asked. "Back from where?"

"I saw you ahead of us, leaving this glen. That's why I stopped George here, and why I thought I had to steal the horse right away."

"You couldn't have seen me," said Christian with a frown.

173

"I was way back in the other direction when I heard the shot."

"How could you be behind us? We were following you!" asserted Margaret, duplicating his frown.

"I got lost."

"But I *saw* you. At least, I saw *something*."

They both looked at the trail's bend ahead. The sun had dipped out of sight, and the narrow clearing was full of shadows. Margaret glanced around the glen with widened eyes. They came to rest among the nearest trees on George's wrapped body. She shuddered, then winced at the pain in her arm.

"If you *had* been ahead," she said slowly, "I might be the one dead, now. What are we going to do with him?"

"Leave him," Christian answered grimly and moved to ready the horse.

"But we can't!" cried Margaret.

"What do you suggest, Margaret?" demanded Christian. "That we take him along for the ride? Or have a funeral?"

Christian had turned to face her again. He was filthy, unshaven, his clothes and hair the color of the dusty road; and Margaret wanted nothing but to throw her arms around him. His eyes softened as he looked at her, along with his tone. "Margaret, there's nothing we can do."

"We couldn't bury him?"

"We have no shovel, and we have no time."

"But Christian, what about the animals out here? They'll . . ."

She lowered her voice almost to a whisper, biting her lip when it began to tremble.

Christian sighed wearily and rubbed the grimy sweat off his forehead. Then he reached out and pulled her carefully into his arms. That tender touch, damp and smelling of horse, brought Margaret close to tears.

"Margaret," he said. "This is war. That body over there is not your old friend. It's the enemy. He was ready to kill us both and be a hero for the king of England. Well, that's what he is — only he's a dead one."

"It seems so wrong," whispered Margaret.

"Death seems wrong," countered Christian. "Betrayal seems wrong. So does fighting because you want peace. But death and betrayal and war are facts. The best we can do is to try to fight well for what's right."

As he spoke, his exhaustion seemed to leave him. Margaret looked at him and saw her brothers with all their ardor for the cause of freedom. She gave the corpse a final, troubled glance, then squared her shoulders.

"I guess we'd better go do it, then," she said.

They traveled due east, looking for the Hudson River beyond the mountainous terrain of the Hudson Highlands.

"Assume nothing," Christian said during one brief rest out of the sun. "We could meet anyone around here: soldier or civilian, friend or foe."

"Well, what do we do, whoever it is?" Margaret asked, as she watched him cleaning his gun and George's, then checking his ammunition. He looked up at her and smiled.

"Just for a start, don't look too pretty," he said and reached out to tug at a damp strand of her hair.

"*That's* no problem," she answered with a glance at her

ruined dress, and the sunburn on her unwrapped arm. "I wish we had some of Mama's soap."

"But I'm serious," Christian continued. "And don't give anything away. We must know who we're dealing with before we tell them anything about us."

"How can we be sure?" she asked. "How long was George a Loyalist before we guessed?"

"Uniforms would be handy, but they aren't everything," he said. "I don't know, Margaret. Pray that we have enough to go on when the time comes."

"But suppose . . ." she began.

"Look, I'll tell you what," said Christian. He laid a hand on her shoulder. "You don't say anything. Just let me handle it."

The moment of confrontation came without any warning. They made their solitary way through the muggy forest morning, expecting only more of the same wilderness trail they'd traveled throughout the Highlands. But suddenly, as though the trees themselves had grown legs and stepped out of their stations, Christian and Margaret found themselves thoroughly surrounded by a group of armed men.

Margaret yelled as they dragged her off the horse and away from Christian, who was taken by another captor. Christian struggled furiously, but two men joined the first who'd grabbed him, making his thrashing useless.

"We're friends!" Christian cried roughly. "We're friends."

Finally, his struggling slowed, then ceased. He stood, hunched tensely between the men, breathing in deep gulps of air. To Margaret, he gasped, "They're Americans. None of the British or German troops look this bad."

Margaret turned from Christian to the men in their hodge-podge uniforms and held her tongue.

"We need to talk to General Wayne," Christian continued. He glanced from one soldier to another, until he finally settled on one man who stood apart. "We have important information for him."

The man asked the others something in English. They shook their heads and muttered among themselves. Then the man turned back to Christian and addressed him in English.

"I don't understand you," said Christian. "Just take us to General Wayne and find someone who knows German. We have to speak to General Wayne."

The man stared at Christian with a frown, then turned to confer again with his companions. The one decipherable constant in the conversation was Wayne's name. Then, the soldiers fell into a formation of sorts, surrounding their prisoners, and proceeded to march them through the woods with one of the men riding ahead on Christian and Margaret's horse, while the rest guarded the captives on foot.

"Are they taking us to the general?" Margaret asked Christian, while the soldiers spoke quiet English around them.

"I don't know," he said. "Don't worry, Margaret. I'll take care of it."

But Christian looked terribly young and worn out, as he trooped along, tripping on an occasional tree root.

The group walked for a half hour before they came to the encampment.

"It's the right army, anyway," he murmured to Margaret.

Their captors led them past groups of soldiers, past the central tents, and on to a number of tiny, windowless huts. Suddenly, Christian yelled and started to thrash and writhe again.

"They're going to lock us up!" he screamed to Margaret.

Immediately, the soldiers were on him full-force, and his struggles accomplished nothing but a ringing clunk on the back of his head when it hit the ground. Margaret started forward, but she too was quickly restrained at some cost to her battered arm.

"Can't you get it straight?" Christian blustered while Margaret's blood pounded in great, fearful rushes through her limbs. "We're friends! We can help! Just let us talk to General Wayne!"

The soldier who held her issued an order, and the others began to drag Christian to his feet and toward the huts.

"Christian!" cried Margaret. "Are you finished handling this yet?"

In the split second that her guard's hold relaxed in surprise, she bent, grabbed up her tattered skirt with her good hand and sprinted for all she was worth. She flew past a group of soldiers and darted around one after another tent, while the hue and cry and the sound of pounding feet gave her wings.

Margaret dashed and dodged, eluding her would-be captors by sheer agility. Finally, when she was all but done in, she saw what she'd been looking for — soldiers in uniforms, *real* uniforms with buttons glinting silver in the sun and lining showing stark white against sun-darkened faces. Uniforms like Jacob's.

She ran headlong into the nearest man, grasped him and held on as though her life depended on it.

"My brother is Captain Jacob Volpert," Margaret gasped, clinging to the man to keep from falling. "Jacob Volpert. He's my brother."

Her knees began to buckle, but she hung on and repeated what she'd said, all the while sucking in huge, burning breaths. Her German *"Bruder"* and Jacob's name must have translated easily. Unlike her captors, this soldier listened carefully, and repeated her phrases after her, even after her pursuers came alongside.

After a short conference with a great commotion of excited English, one of the soldiers took off at a quick trot, while the rest of the group stood and waited. Margaret's breathing had slowed. She stepped away from her rescuer with a *"danke schön"* and waited as well.

Chapter Ten

I

Christian found Margaret at the door of the detention hut with her brother as he emerged, blinking in the bright daylight. At the sight of Jacob, he sagged with relief. Then he turned to Margaret. Perspiration beaded and dripped across her grimy forehead and cheeks, and her tattered dress hung loose. But she smiled broadly at Christian, and it made him catch his breath.

"Good job," he said and matched her smile. "*Danke.*"

Soon, the trio walked together through the encampment, sharing salty rations and explaining themselves.

"You two are unbelievably lucky," Jacob was saying. "You could as easily have roamed into British hands as ours. You might have ended up on one of their prison ships and never have been heard of again!"

"Why wouldn't they take us to Wayne?" asked Christian.

"We've all been instructed to clear the countryside of

wanderers, Christian," he said. "Something is up. I'm surprised giving my name did any good."

"It was all I could think of," said Margaret with a shrug that made her gasp and grab her arm.

"You," said Jacob sternly, "have a *lot* to explain."

The first business, however, took the informers to Jacob's commander. They stood before the famous man, his fine ruffled uniform making their rags the more wretched, and at last related Christian's intelligence. Jacob translated, then gave his assurance of them as reliable, while "Mad Anthony" listened closely, tapping his knee with his riding crop and scrutinizing them as though to read their souls. Their tale completed, he abruptly, though cordially, invited them to leave the tent.

"Well," said Christian, as they waited outside for Jacob. "That's that."

"I guess so," agreed Margaret.

"I hope it's helpful."

"Me, too."

And they both sighed.

In the days that followed, Margaret stayed with some army wives, while Christian was bunked with Jacob's own company. A camp doctor set Margaret's arm with a proper splint and a sling, then bled her. She took a day recovering from his cure and was considerably more comfortable after that.

When Jacob invited Christian to drill with the troops, he readily agreed.

"For old times' sake," he said.

How natural it felt to be back in training! He wished John could see him.

On Sunday, the troops with their women and children gathered to hear the chaplains preach. The German-American minister rallied the Light Infantry's German-speaking members.

"Our great God commands us to lift the sword to establish peace," he said, "to protect innocence, secure our liberties, and humble the proud tyrants of the earth."

"He sounds just like Reverend Stern in Reading," whispered Margaret.

"Of the righteousness of our cause, there can be no doubt," the man continued. "We can be certain that God will be on our side. And if the Lord is for us, what can men do unto us?"

Christian listened as never before. Always, he had considered the soldier's business in terms of his Prussian duty to his prince, who had the power to demand his services. Then he had fallen into the hands of the "rebels" and met the Volperts. In their company, he discovered that it was possible to fight, not for duty's sake, but in order to right terrible wrongs. Now this chaplain spoke of the command and blessing of God and his words swept through Christian like a fiery wind.

"Can I conclude my address to you without solemnly blessing you in the name of the God of our fathers!" the chaplain continued. "May he be with you and keep you at all times in the hollow of his hand! May he cover your heads in the battles to come, and enable you to play the men for your families and the people of America! Amen."

Christian glanced at Jacob, sitting a short distance ahead

of him — Jacob, who had given himself to this army and its cause, just as John had. Then Christian looked at Margaret sitting beside him. A small boy sat cradled on her lap, sucking his thumb, while she stroked his head. But her attention seemed focused entirely on the preacher, and as he pronounced his benediction with its resounding "Amen," Christian thought she was set aglow by the same searing breath that he felt.

After dinner that day, Margaret and Christian strolled by the Hudson. A cloudy morning fulfilled its promise of rain, and they stood for a long time watching it play on the wide surface of the river.

"Jacob says he's written to your parents," Christian said. He glanced at Margaret beside him. The morning's glow was gone. She was once again the Margaret he knew so well. "He told them he'd see to your return when it was possible."

"You could take me back," suggested Margaret. "We managed rather well until the Continental Army caught up with us."

She smiled, but Christian felt a lump in his throat, and looked away. When he continued, he stared out over the water with his arms folded in front of him.

"I asked Jacob to write for me as well," he said. A short silence ensued. Finally Margaret interrupted the pattering quiet in a soft voice.

"About John's injury?" she asked.

Christian nodded.

"So you told Jacob," said Margaret. "What did he say?"

"That it was an amazing coincidence," said Christian. "And that I must feel terrible. Then he said it was a bad

183

idea to tell your parents; that it could only serve to hurt them, because even though I wounded John as a stranger and an enemy, it was still my doing. Every time they saw me, it would remind them of his death."

Margaret, who had turned somber over the mention of John, brightened again at Christian's last statement.

"Oh, Christian," she said and laid her hand on his arm. "You will come back to Reading, won't you? I wanted to tell you that the day you left, and to tell you to stop blaming yourself."

"Well, I could see Jacob's point," Christian said. He covered Margaret's hand with his own and swallowed hard to clear his throat. "He did write something else for me, though."

Margaret waited with an encouraging nod.

"Margaret, I asked your father for permission to address you formally."

Christian concentrated on the river's endless movement in the long pause that followed. Then Margaret burst into full-voiced laughter.

"Christian, you idiot!" she said. "Why not just ask *me*?"

Christian drew himself up to his full height, all at once feeling thoroughly German.

"My affection for you is honorable, Margaret," he said solemnly. Margaret blinked at that, and assumed a chastened expression. "Honor required that I speak to your father."

"I beg your pardon. Of course, that was most proper of you," she said with dignity to match Christian's. But a twinkle sneaked back into her eyes. "We might have to wait awhile before we hear from Papa, though."

"Actually," he confessed, while his face grew warm, "Jacob considered your father's permission a formality." Christian cleared his throat again nervously. "He said he deems himself your guardian for as long as you're here. So he's given me permission on behalf of your father."

"Oh," said Margaret. She gazed up at Christian in obvious anticipation. "Well, then."

Christian stared at her and saw in her frank response a person he hardly knew, after all.

Then, in spite of the change and maybe because of it, too, Christian went on to make his feelings for Margaret unmistakably clear, without the least formality or shyness in the world.

That evening, they stood together outside her tent, saying *guten Abend*.

"I'm probably unwelcome," sounded Jacob's voice from the shadows. He came alongside them. "I'm here in an official capacity."

"As guardian?" asked Margaret and chuckled.

"No," answered her brother with a smile. "As company commander."

"Is something wrong?" asked Christian.

"I would say not," said Jacob. "But I'll let you judge. General Wayne has offered you a place in my division, if you want it; in thanks for your service."

"A place?" Christian repeated slowly.

"You mean the general wants to make Christian a Continental soldier?" Margaret asked in a strained voice.

"If Christian wants it," said Jacob, watching Christian. "I have to tell you, Molitor. This is quite an honor. No new recruits have been allowed here. These troops are hand-picked, highly trained, and on the verge of something big. Wayne's offer is a high commendation."

Now Christian stared from one blue, Volpert gaze to the other, and he remembered another's like them. His hand went to his chest. He felt, as he so often did, John's gold coin under his borrowed shirt, and heard again John's ringing assertion — "It's a place good enough to die for . . . we have the right to be free." He closed his hand firmly around the coin, then extended the other to Jacob.

"I accept the honor," he said. "With thanks."

Jacob took Christian's hand and shook it gravely. Then, without dropping their handclasp, the two men looked at Margaret. For one moment, she held back, with an almost unbearable expression of sadness. Then she took a deep breath and added her hand to the men's.

II

On the morning of July 15, 1779, the entire Light Infantry Corps assembled for inspection. The barest breeze skimmed to the top of the trees, but left the air on the ground untouched and breathless.

"Last night, the third and fourth regiments came in to Sandy Beach to join us," Jacob said at breakfast. "Now all of us, probably thirteen hundred men, have been ordered up for inspection. Something's going on."

After that, Margaret stuck close to Christian and her

brother while they got ready. When Christian was shaved, and his hair tied back and powdered with flour, she watched him pack his equipment and rations in his backpack and cartouche.

"Why is everyone packing?" Margaret asked. She cradled her broken arm in her good one the way she had the child on Sunday morning. "This is just an inspection, right?"

"We'll be checked for battle readiness," said Christian. "I'm only ready for battle when I have everything I need *on* me."

"You look different," said Margaret. "I've never seen you in uniform before."

"You still haven't seen him in a uniform," said Jacob as he passed with supplies. He shook his head as he scanned the bustling soldiers around them, many in ill-assorted costumes. "To look at us, you'd never guess we belong to each other."

Margaret still stared at Christian and he suddenly found himself smiling, a contagious grin that Margaret caught in spite of herself.

"All right, men," ordered Jacob. "Fall in. Let's move out."

Christian and Margaret clasped hands, then he pulled her into a tight embrace that she returned with energy.

"You look wonderful," she asserted. She shrugged her head in the direction of the parade ground. "I'll be watching you out there."

Jacob came alongside the pair and clapped Christian smartly on the back.

"Come on, friend," he said. "This is your first real appearance. You don't want to be late for the party."

"Yes, sir," said Christian with his smile back in place. He gave Margaret a sudden kiss full on her mouth that left her rosy-cheeked and made Jacob roll his eyes.

"We'll see you at dinner," Christian called over his shoulder as they moved away.

"I'll be waiting," Margaret called back with a wave.

The field of men and horses seemed to shimmer and dance in the beating sun. General Wayne paraded up and down on his horse, reviewing row after row of carefully groomed, if oddly dressed, men. "Mad Anthony" did not overpower in size or good looks, not like George Washington. But what he lacked in physical attraction, he more than made up for in animation. The air seemed to crackle as he passed.

When Wayne had ridden off, the troops waited under the noonday sun for dismissal. But when the order came, it was not to break ranks. It was to march.

Christian exchanged startled glances with the men around him. Jacob raised his eyebrows and gave Christian a wink, then called his division into marching order and moved them out. As they marched, Christian searched the open ground on either side of the column of troops. At the last possible moment, he finally caught sight of Margaret among the camp followers. She waved frantically and shouted something, but the noise of more than a thousand marching men and the clatter of equipment made it impossible to hear her. He could only raise his weapon in farewell and wish her a silent safekeeping. "I'll be waiting," she had said earlier. Christian would depend on it.

No one knew where they were going or for what, not even the field officers. Some of the men passed the time speculating, a few laying wagers on opposing guesses.

"Can't be any of the Hudson forts," said one soldier behind Christian. "We're marching away from the river."

"This is the hard way to get *anywhere*," added another as they picked their way through some boggy underbrush. "It doesn't make sense."

How often had Christian passed the time this way, with the army he now marched against? But as the afternoon blazed, the guessing game faded. Christian marched to the beat of his own sober reflections: Were they marching to an assault? Would many fall before it was over? And who, in the end, would emerge the victor?

They marched for four stifling miles through the mountains before they were ordered to stop and refresh themselves. When they resumed their trek, the damp heat and the unfriendly terrain fought their every step. Still they pressed on, according to orders, often in single file because the trail was so poor.

Christian said little. He'd had less than a week with Jacob's company, and many of the men were faces without names. Yet, how different from his reception in the Bethlehem hospital! The soldier beside him offered a piece of salt beef to chew while they trudged, and another took turns with him, holding back the snapping brambles to allow passage.

Not until eight o'clock that evening, when darkness nagged at the eastern horizon and the forest twinkled with fireflies, did the Light Infantry finally come to rest. According to Jacob, they had marched thirteen miles. Only now, at the cooling end of that grueling hike, was its purpose finally revealed.

The corps, in their several companies, stood at attention while they received their orders.

"About a mile and a half on the other side of this hill," said the commander, pointing at the rising ground to their east, "is Stony Point. The fortress is formidable, but not impregnable. Our intelligence has discovered a soft spot that we can exploit with the element of surprise."

Christian exchanged a lightheaded glance with Jacob.

"Tonight, at midnight," the officer continued, "we will attack the fort from two sides. There will be no muskets used — only bayonets. Our goal is total secrecy. To succeed, we must advance all the way inside the fort, *without being seen or heard*. It's our only hope of victory, because the British have every advantage otherwise."

He went on to describe the approach, which would be made from three angles — two real assaults and one decoy attack between them. As he spoke, the troops stood in perfect silence, the same silence they'd be expected to maintain throughout the assault. The air was charged with their mounting tension.

"I need twenty volunteers to form our 'forlorn hope,'" said the commander. "That group will lead the way. They will have to tear down the first defenses and silence anyone who gets in their way."

If the atmosphere had been tense before, it was pulsating now. Assignment to the forlorn hope was easily the most dangerous mission of the assault. It was also the most important. The success of the whole attack could depend on those twenty men who led and cleared the way.

The colonel was calling for volunteers. Christian stared at his hands in the violet light of evening and compulsively reached for John's coin. "It's a place worth dying for," he seemed to hear. "We have a right to be free." Almost before he himself knew what he was going to do, Christian stepped forward out of rank. He looked neither right nor left, but he knew without a doubt that he stood as the first volunteer for the job.

III

A half hour short of moonlit midnight, Christian joined the march back to the Hudson River, heading for the south end of Stony Point's island. Only the two decoy companies under Major Murfree, who would approach the island directly, carried loaded muskets to open fire and distract the British at the moment of surprise attack.

"I want to load my gun," one soldier said to Christian as they were moving out. "I don't understand fighting without shooting."

The look in his eye was like that of a cornered animal. And he wasn't the only man who objected to carrying an empty weapon. But the colonel had made it clear.

"Any man who presumes to fire his musket before he's ordered to, shall be instantly put to death by the officer next to him," he warned. "The misconduct of one man won't be allowed to put the entire troops in danger."

Christian felt the tumultuous churning of his stomach as he adjusted his only tools: a bayonet, a billhook, and an ax. They seemed paltry in the face of imminent battle. Tremors of excitement ran along every nerve and tendon of his body — just as they had that morning when he'd realized that the second volunteer for the forlorn hope was none other than Jacob Volpert.

After twenty minutes' marching, Major Murfree's diversionary troops broke off to establish their position. The whole operation proceeded with uncanny quiet in the warm, sticky night. The rumors that advance scouts had killed all the local dogs to insure secrecy seemed plausible.

Ahead, Christian caught his first sight of Stony Point rising like a rocky shrug in the landscape before the troops' advance. Before it lay the marsh that made Stony Point a high-tide island. Slips of white paper were passed among the men, along with a last, whispered reminder to use only bayonets. Christian fixed the paper, meant to distinguish him from the enemy in the midnight battle, to his hat. He gazed up at the fort's promontory. He could see some of the cannons and defenses in place, and they looked murderous. But no enemy pickets appeared.

We'll need every advantage we can get, he thought. What had the chaplain said? "Since our cause is just, we can be certain that God will be on our side." Christian hoped with all his heart the man was right. Those words had filled him with confidence when he sat safely among the troops at Sandy Beach. They were less convincing at midnight on Stony Point.

The troops moved forward into the marshland with Christian, Jacob, and the forlorn hope in the lead. As they walked into the tall swamp weeds, Christian felt his boots fill with water. An image of the battle at Brandywine Creek flashed across his mind, while the wet crept up his legs to his waist. What was this? The slogging progress through the water was taking too long! It was making too much noise!

A whisper sighed past Christian's ear.

"The tide," someone muttered under his breath. "The damned tide is in!"

At that moment a shot rang out over their heads. They'd been spotted from the fort! The tide had betrayed them; battle was joined!

Christian threw himself through the water, his gun held high, until the tangling marsh grass gave way to the tumble of rocks at Stony Point's base. Then, slinging the musket over his shoulder, he began the savage scramble, with his ax and billhook, into the enemy's lap.

They came to the first line of abatis and, with a single will, attacked the pile-up of logs and felled trees like a pack of wolves, ravaging the spiky works as though it were the carcass from a successful hunt. Chips of bark and wood showered around them, stinging Christian's face and eyes as he hacked and wrenched at the defenses. As the first abatis was cleared, the explosion of cannon fire hurried the forlorn hope all the more. They scrambled over the wreckage, trading axes for muskets with bayonets fixed.

As Jacob and Christian plunged ahead, the soldier just in front of them suddenly jerked wildly to one side and fell, first victim of British fire. Then a man to their left went down with a choking yell. Christian clenched his teeth hard against rising panic and pushed on. He could still hear some of the men chopping frantically at the abatis to clear a passage for the troops, while wave after wave of Americans clambered over and through.

Sounds of gunfire from the north competed with what was just above them.

"Murfree is in place!" shouted Jacob. "We're on our way."

From behind them, someone else shouted.

"Wayne is down! They got Wayne!"

Christian faltered, but Jacob pushed ahead, heedless of the cries around him, and the Hessian moved to keep pace. At the top of the fort, Christian could see a break in the wall. Others spotted it, too, and though the British called out on all sides, the Americans wouldn't be stopped as they pressed upward into the teeth of their enemy.

Sweat was pouring down Christian's face, and making his hands slick. He tripped and fell against Jacob.

"What are they saying?" he screamed over the tumult around them, as they righted themselves.

" 'Come on, you damned rebels, come on!' " Jacob translated. Then he called out in reply, "Don't be in such a hurry, we'll be with you presently!"

Christian grinned, but only for a moment, for Jacob had surged ahead again, waving him and the others on frantically.

"Sally port ahead!" he cried and vanished through the break in the defenses, with Christian right behind him. Directly before them was a low wall and they threw themselves over. At last, the summit of the fort stretched in front of them. They were in! Someone roared in triumph, "The fort is ours!"

American troops poured in at the sally port, then veered to right and left, to surround the summit. On all sides, men clashed in hand-to-hand combat. The moments between life and death could be measured in seconds.

Christian battled alongside Jacob with the power of a lunatic, pushing to close the circle of the fort's summit and watching on every side for attack. Just then, a British rifleman appeared at Jacob's back. He raised his gun and readied to fire, but Christian was on him like a man possessed. With one vicious stroke of his rifle butt, he dropped Jacob's would-be killer. Jacob battled forward through the skirmish, without knowing that Christian stayed close behind, like a loyal watchdog, ready to fend off all attacks.

This time, Christian vowed, the Volpert soldier would return unharmed.

No sooner had he thought this than he found himself facing a small group of British soldiers who were throwing down their arms and crying, "Mercy, mercy, dear Americans; quarter, quarter!" That was English he understood perfectly, and he stood to attention, his bayonet at guard.

Suddenly, all around them, the British who hadn't surrendered were running in every direction. One by one, they ran into the arms of the "rebels" and begged "mercy."

A commotion to his rear drew Christian's attention. As he looked, he saw a British colonel being led away under guard.

"Who is it?" he called to a passing German-American.

"Colonel Johnson, commander of the fort," the man cried. At the same time, a ground swell of American cheers began, grew, and expanded until they filled the night air like the roar of a hundred cannon. Troops who had entered by the northern approach began to flood into that end of the summit. The British were caught. The mighty fortress at Stony Point had fallen for the cause of freedom.

Amid the din, Jacob shook Christian's arm and pointed to where the flagpole stood by the western rampart. An American soldier was shinnying up while his comrades bellowed beneath him. As he climbed, a small contingent of American officers approached to stand below. Christian recognized General Anthony Wayne among them. He held a bloodied bandage to his forehead, and men supported him on both sides.

Meanwhile, the soldier at the top of the pole had grabbed the British standard, and with his shortknife, cut away the rope that held it in place. He ripped the flag free and held it aloft to the triumphant roar of his fellow troops.

As he did, Jacob Volpert joined his hand to Christian's, and in exactly the same gesture, raised their joined hands to heaven.

Epilogue

Margaret closed the kitchen door behind her. She could hear through its thick planks the musical rise and fall of celebration in progress, festivity she had shared gladly throughout the day. But now, in its last hours, she left its magic without regret as she felt another, more compelling, pull.

The icy ground crunched under Margaret's feet as she crossed the yard to the shop, and unlatched the door. How often had she done this in the last year and a half, she wondered, groping her way to the table lantern and flint? It hissed, as always, but by now she hardly noticed. Before she even sat at her father's desk, she was composing the lines that would open her latest weekly epistle to the war front.

She prepared pen and ink, drew a sheet of thick paper before her, and began, with much labor and many pauses, to write.

24 December 1781

Dear Christian,

It is Christmas Eve, and I wonder what you and Jacob are doing right now. How we missed you both today! Elizabeth Scheffer made a clumsy Pelznickel and little Johann Mumberg cried, but otherwise all was just as it should be — if only we had sugar for the cakes, and you beside us.

"Captain" Mama says I must order you to arrange a furlough soon (as though I need her encouragement!) because she has made you both something wonderful for your winter encampment. She said I mustn't tell you what, but I will. She knitted you each a heavy wool vest for under your uniform (don't ask wherever she found wool, she'll never tell). Yours is the handsomer, I believe. Christian, you must never be sorry we haven't told her about John. She loves you so, it's almost as though you were a new son to her.

Papa is making plans to add two rooms off the shop for us. He'll begin after the thaw and he is convinced you'll be home in time to help. Maybe the church won't be a hospital anymore and we can be married there. Do you suppose the war will be over by then? How I pray for it! I spend most of every day at the courthouse

hospital, and the thought of an endless number
of men in such condition breaks my heart.

Now that the war has moved south, Reading
wants to forget that it exists. But some of us will
never forget until we have our men home to stay,
and freedom secured.

Aren't I learning my writing lessons well?
I'm glad, but I'll be happy for less reason for
practice. Do try to hurry home, even for a short
visit. All the family sends their love. But most of
all, Christian, I send you mine.

> *Auf Wiedersehen,*
> *Margaret*

Margaret sat until the shop's chill became unbearable, staring at her letter and remembering as she often did the first letter she'd read in this lantern's light — the letter Christian left when he rode to Stony Point.

Like a small break in a great dam, that recollection started a flood of memories as Margaret thought back on the Revolution and the suffering it had exacted from the Volpert family. The cost of independence was steep: one brother dead and another bound in service with poor provisions; a marriage postponed; a childhood friend killed for aiding the enemy; and nameless hundreds who never survived the agony of the Moravian hospital, the courthouse hospital in Reading, and the many other makeshift facilities throughout the colonies.

At the thought of the hospitals, Margaret shuddered. Was it worth it? Was independence worth the killings, horror, and suffering she had witnessed and experienced? With that thought, another image rose in her mind. She saw, out of a past now distant by years, a beautiful bird — a broad-winged hawk — soaring over the Pennsylvania countryside and riding the winds from cloud to cloud.

"He's free," she thought. "And we will be, too."

Note

The story of Christian Molitor and the Volpert family is fiction. The main characters never lived, except in the pages of *An Enemy Among Them*. But people like them lived — Germans and German-Americans in similar circumstances, and with the same fears, hopes, and conflicts. All the places, such as Reading, the Moravian Brethren's House in Bethlehem, and Stony Point, existed as described at the time of the American Revolution. The battles, too, actually happened and included Pennsylvania Germans and Hessians.

Two people wrote *An Enemy Among Them*; one is a fiction writer for young people; the other is a historian who writes for scholars and adults. Together, we wrote this historical novel for young people. The historian provided the factual material and an expert's understanding of what it all meant, and the novelist set out to tell an imaginary story based on that material. Through the novel, we hoped readers would understand more about history, people, and themselves.

The facts about Revolutionary Pennsylvania come from many sources. The people who lived through that time sometimes left behind letters and diaries, maps and town records with names, occupations, and inventories of belongings. Soldiers' orderly books have been preserved, as well as newspapers, drawings, and actual household items. We owe special thanks to Karen Guenther, a doctoral candidate at the University of Connecticut, who spent part of a summer combing through records and lists for us in Reading, Pennsylvania. We looked at far more material than finally appears in *An Enemy Among Them*, but all of it contributed to our ability to tell a *true* fictional story.

For readers who would like to know more about Pennsylvania during the Revolution, or about the Germans who came to America, a number of nonfiction works are available. For instance, Rodney Atwood's *The Hessians: Mercenaries from Hessen-Kassel in the American Revolution* tells the story from the Hessian soldiers' perspective. Sol Stember takes a different approach in *The Bicentennial Guide to the American Revolution: The Middle Colonies*. In his guide, Stember describes his own travels over the physical landscape of the war as it now exists.

William P. Cummings and Hugh F. Rankin have written a colorful, more general book about the colonies during the American Revolution, using many actual documents from the time, *The Fate of a Nation: The American Revolution Through Contemporary Eyes*. This is especially interesting because much of the material is in the words of people who lived and wrote during the Revolutionary War. In their accounts, we begin to understand what made each of their lives unique. We also learn one of history's most fundamental lessons — how much we all have in common.

D. H. D. and H. S. S.